Familiar Spirit

Familiar Way Book 2

by A.M.Burns

Copyright 2017 © MysticHawker Press
http://www.mystichawker.com/

ISBN: 978-1-945632-12-9

Cover design by Photos for Books

To Sandy Stevens.

Thanks for all the wonderful ideas and tons of support over the years.

1

Long Weekend

The final bell sounded, releasing Lugh McNeal from the mind-numbing boredom of his algebra class. Shoving his textbook and homework into his backpack, he joined the growing stream of students heading for freedom. He paused at the door to class and glanced back over his shoulder. His gray hoodie still hung from the back of his chair. A frustrated groan escaped him as he turned in the tide to go back for it. *How long is it going to take me to remember jackets? I didn't have to have jackets in Florida.* Getting used to life in Steamboat Springs, Colorado was more than just getting used to a higher elevation and a new town. It was a whole new way of life.

He yanked his hoodie from the chair and realized that the room was now empty except for Mr. Lester, the math teacher. Without a word to the teacher, Lugh hurried out.

"Hey, Lugh!" Wyn Chambers called as Lugh stepped into the rapidly emptying hall. "There you are."

Lugh smiled at Wyn, his boyfriend and the hottest guy in school, at least in his opinion. "Hey, Wyn. Yeah, I left my jacket again."

"You'll get it figured out. At least this time you didn't end up having to check the lost and found box in the office."

"There is that." Lugh nodded as he fell into step with Wyn, walking toward the main doors of Steamboat Springs High School. Wyn helped make Lugh's transition to the new school a lot easier.

"I got a text from Dad, right after the bell rang." Wyn stopped to open his locker, a couple of spots down from Lugh's. "He's got everything ready to go. Once we get to the shop, he'll drive us up to the camp site."

As he opened his own locker, Lugh's heart raced. They'd been trying to plan a camping trip for almost two months. Things always seemed to come up to keep them from going and Wyn said if they didn't make it soon, they'd have to wait until spring. The aspen leaves already showed gold and red around their edges and the temperatures were noticeably chillier than they had been a month earlier.

"Cool." Lugh stashed several books he wasn't going to need and closed the small metal door. "We've got to stop by Sacred Paths to get Bran. Did he say if he'd stopped by my house yet for my stuff? Last night, I piled everything near the front door so Mom could find it."

Wyn shrugged. "He didn't say, but if he hasn't your house isn't too far off the route up the mountain."

They started back toward door.

"Hey, you two, still going camping this weekend?" Lugh's cousin, Abby Ballor, appeared from the girls' bathroom nearest the front doors. She had an annoying habit of just popping up out of nowhere, almost like magic.

"Yeah." Lugh had been hoping to get out of town without dealing with his cousin even though the chances were minor, particularly since they had to stop by the shop her mother, Lugh's Aunt Catherine, owned to get Lugh's familiar, Bran. Lugh, Abby and Catherine were Magi, people gifted with the ability to manipulate the forces of magic in the world. Their familiars amplified the amount of power they controlled. Without their animal companions, they couldn't control as much magic, and even risked going insane. It was a strange and wonderful world—one Lugh was still getting used to.

"I'm surprised Bran isn't throwing more of a fit about that." Abby fell into step with the two boys. "I know Morrigan wouldn't like it at all if I decided I was going to go camping for the weekend."

Lugh didn't bother informing Abby that he and Bran, his gray cat, had been discussing the impending journey into the wilderness for several weeks. Bran was still young, and Lugh had finally convinced him that it was going to be an adventure. But he still expected to hear a lot of complaining coming through the telepathic link he shared with his familiar.

"Bran's resigned to the idea," Wyn said for Lugh. "From what I can tell, they've had some fairly lengthy discussions. But Bran's down with it."

Abby shook her head, her long red hair waved around her as they walked outside and the still north breeze caught it. "Must be the difference between boys and girls. Morrigan'd gripe at me all the way there and back."

"Well then, I guess I should be happy I didn't bond with a girl cat," Lugh said. For a second, he debated putting on his hoodie. But, the cool wind didn't seem to affect Wyn or Abby, so he left it dangling over his arm. He didn't like appearing wimpy in front of Wyn.

For a second Abby pursed her lips. "I can't say as I recall, other than Henry and Matilda, anyone bonding with a familiar of the opposite sex. Mom says that birds of prey are odd that way."

Lugh nodded but didn't reply. He'd met Henry Claiborne and his familiar Matilda, the goshawk, two months before, at a gathering of Magi up in the mountains. He would never forget that night. It had been his first real experience with magic. That night he'd gotten the ring that allowed him to focus his magic, and Abby had shown him the magical paths that all Magi could use to travel around, unseen by the rest of the world. Sure, dark forces attacked them, but the cool parts outweighed the scary bits.

"Now, that's interesting to know," Wyn said. "Especially for us non-Magi types."

"Even for us newer Magi," Lugh added. Wyn might not be a Magus, his family followed the old ways and understood magic, even if it didn't work the same way for them that it did for Magi. A lot of the things that Catherine and Abby taught Lugh about magic were similar to things Wyn's family did, but with much more concrete and dramatic results.

As they paused waiting for the crosswalk signal to change, Abby frowned at Lugh. "I'm pretty sure that Mom covered that with you." She shook her head. "I do wish your mother had let your father explain magical life to you like my mom did me. You'd be much further along by now."

"I'm just thankful that Mom's letting me learn about it at all." Lugh stepped off the curb as the red hand of the crosswalk signal vanished, replaced by a green person with a countdown under it.

"She'd be more upset about it if she knew about the Dark Magi," Wyn said.

Lugh sighed sadly as he stepped up on the curb on the far side of the street. "Yeah." They hadn't heard anything about new dark magi in town since he and Bran defeated the ones who kidnapped Abby and Wyn two months before. They had kept the incident from his mother, since she still had reservations about Lugh learning magic, even if the alternative was him going insane as his powers bloomed. It was one of those things even his Aunt Catherine had agreed with, although none of them liked the idea of lying to his mother.

"So, when will you guys be back from camping?" Abby changed the subject. Even knowing that Lugh talked to Wyn about Magi stuff, she tended to change the subject when they wondered onto it with her around. Lugh no longer got mad at her about it. It was just Abby being Abby.

"Dad's supposed to pick us up Monday," Wyn said. "Unless the weather turns nasty, then he'll come back for us sooner. I guess we can thank a teacher-in-service-day for the extra day."

Abby shrugged her narrow shoulders. "Anything for a three-day weekend. Even if we do get Samhain off, we can always use a few more days away from school."

"Okay, another term I don't know," Lugh said. Abby and Wyn, more Abby though, always seemed to be coming up with new terms.

"Most folks call it Halloween," she replied. The note of superiority, that often colored her voice when she knew something he didn't, crept in. "Samhain is one of the high holy days for us."

"Like Lughnasadh?" Lugh asked. He'd met Wyn, Bran and Abby on Lughnasadh, which happened to be the same day as his birthday.

Wyn nodded as they stopped for the next cross street. "Exactly. It's one of the times of the year when the veil between the living world and the underworld is the thinnest. We take the time to honor those that have passed beyond the veil."

An idea hit Lugh as he digested what Wyn said. "So does this mean that we'll be doing something to honor my dad then?" It was only a couple of weeks away.

Abby shot Lugh a strange glance that he couldn't interpret. "That'll be up to my mom and yours. I suppose, if they don't do something, we could do something ourselves." Then a bright gleam lit up her green eyes. "You know, that might be kinda cool. If we did something just us, it would mean I'd get to be high priestess for the first time. That'd be cool. But we better wait and see what everyone else has planned. I know we'll be meeting up with the other magi at midnight that night."

"When we get back from camping, we'll have to figure something out," Wyn said.

"You know this *will* be Magi stuff." Abby glared at him.

"Hey, if it's not something really magical, I want Wyn there." For a second, Lugh had the urge to reach out and take Wyn's hand, but he resisted. Steamboat Springs might be fairly open, but they kept public displays of affection to a minimum. They didn't want to invite trouble.

"Especially if it's just us," Wyn added.

Abby huffed as they stopped outside the door to Sacred Paths Metaphysical Shop. "If it's just us, I suppose it will be okay."

"Good." Lugh stepped around Abby and pushed the door to the shop open. The unique smell of incense, candles and herbs hit him as he walked through the door. A faint tingle brushed along his skin. The first time he'd walked into the store, the sensation startled him. Now, he knew it was the protective magical shields his aunt placed around the shop to keep negative energies out.

"Ah, there you three are," Catherine Ballor said from behind the cash register.

"We're right on time," Abby said.

Her mother nodded. "Yes." She smiled at them. "One of these days, you'll understand why parents are always happy to see their children, especially when you're all on time."

"I can't stick around today," Lugh said. "I just stopped by to grab Bran and we're heading up into the mountains to go camping."

"I remembered," his aunt replied. "Last time I saw Bran he was asleep on the shelf in the back with the other cats."

"Thanks." Lugh headed through the brightly colored, beaded curtain that separated the back room from the rest of the shop. The lone light bulb barely provided enough light to see by. On the far wall, in the middle of the otherwise cluttered shelves, a multi-colored pile of fur shifted as three cats looked up at him.

"Is it that time already?" Bran's mental voice rang in Lugh head as the gray cat yawned, but didn't otherwise move. *"I'm in the middle of my third nap this afternoon. Don't you think you could go get everything ready and then stop back by here and get me on your way out of town?"*

Lugh smiled at his familiar. "Nope, time for you to get moving. I'd like to get the tent set up before the sun goes down. It's Wyn's tent, so I want to see how it goes up."

Bran stood up and stretched over Morrigan and Bast. *"If you insist. You know, I'm okay with putting off our adventure for a while."* Since he'd bonded with Lugh, the kitten had grown considerably and was now almost as large as his mother, Bast.

"Nope." Lugh shook his head. "If we don't go this weekend, Wyn says it will probably be too cold to go until spring."

"And you're sure I'm not going to get cold while we're camping?" Bran jumped off the shelf and walked over to Lugh.

Lugh shrugged. "I can't guarantee that. Wyn keeps reminding me that this is Colorado, and the weather forecasts are less accurate than tarot cards."

Bran glared as he strolled past Lugh and through the beaded curtain into the front of the shop. *"That's not reassuring."*

Not bothering to reply, Lugh followed the cat. "I guess we're ready," he announced.

Catherine walked over and gave him a big hug. "Keep your cell phone on in case you need something. Also, remember if something happens, there are air paths all over the mountains. They might be small and hard to find, but they are there."

"I'll remember. But hopefully nothing's going to happen. We're just going a few miles outside of town." Lugh glanced at Wyn. "Right?"

Wyn nodded. "Yep, up near the pass."

"I'll be thinking of you while I'm nice and warm here," Abby said.

"Just have fun and be safe," Catherine said.

Lugh paused as Wyn opened the door for him and Bran. For a moment, it felt like he was leaving his new family members for longer than just the weekend. Over the past months, he hadn't gone a day without seeing Catherine and Abby. He swallowed back the sudden fear that he might not see them again. "We will."

A. M. Burns

2

Setting up Camp

"You boys are sure you're going to be okay, all weekend?" Bryan Chambers, Wyn's father asked for the third time since they arrived at their camp. It was a well-used spot with permanent fire rings and sparse grass showing lots of bare spots where people often pitched tents. Wyn had explained to Lugh when they planned their weekend, that it was a spot his father and some of the other mountain outfitters often started their long wilderness excursions from.

"We'll be fine, Dad," Wyn replied.

"You know, I don't think he would mind if we got back in the truck and rode back down to town," Bran said, looking around dubiously. *"What are we going to do if it rains?"*

Lugh glared at the cat as he sat his backpack down next to the nearest fire ring. "Bran's already complaining about getting wet."

Wyn chuckled as he moved an armload of chopped wood from the back of the truck. "He's a cat, of course he's worried about getting wet. But I thought we worked through his fears of water."

"I'm not afraid," Bran replied. *"I simply don't wish to get wet. There is a difference."*

Laughing, Lugh relayed the cat's thoughts.

Bryan Chambers looked around. "Make sure no one hears you talk about listening to the cat. It's still a bit much to take in and I'm Wiccan."

"We know, Dad." Wyn dropped another armload of wood in the quickly growing pile. "We keep a lot of things quiet." Wyn gave Lugh a knowing wink. Both Wyn's folks and Lugh's mom knew they were dating, but they had been warned to keep their relationship low key outside of family and close friends. Even in an open-minded area like Steamboat Springs there was still the chance one of their classmates might be harboring some fears or hatred they weren't prepared to face.

"If you run into trouble, there's cell signal up here since the highway is only a couple miles down the hill. Call if you need *anything.*" Bryan looked at Lugh. "Wyn's mom and I talked with your mother. If either one of us doesn't get a call each night, I'm coming up here to bring you boys home. Do I make myself clear?"

Lugh nodded as he started helping Wyn unload the wood. "Yes, Mr. Cham...Bryan." He was always doing what he could to make sure both his mom and Wyn's folks stayed happy with them. Neither of them wanted to be forced to sneak around if their parents decided to interfere with their relationship.

Wyn let out a heavy sigh. "Yes, Dad."

Negotiating with the parents had been one of the biggest hurdles they had faced in getting to have their weekend camping trip. Although his mom and the Chambers trusted them, there had been some concerns about letting them out alone for a weekend. Most of it had to do with what other people might think. But the two had promised to not go on any of the more difficult hiking trails, do their best to avoid the wildlife, and not get into any trouble. It was only the fact Wyn had been camping in the mountains since before he could walk, that convinced Lugh's mom he'd be safe. As a family, he'd been camping on the beaches in Florida several times, but it wasn't something his mother enjoyed, so it worried her. Not to mention the mountains of Colorado were vastly different from the beaches he'd grown up with. He knew if he didn't check in every night, she'd be even more worried.

"Your mother packed everything you should need in the way of food, Wyn," Bryan continued.

"I know. She went over it with me last night." Wyn dropped his last armload of wood by the fire pit. "We'll be fine."

"And you've got your fire starting kit?"

Wyn rolled his eyes. "Yes, Dad. I've got the fire starting kit, and even if I didn't, Catherine taught Lugh how to start fires a couple of weeks ago. We'll be warm and have hot food."

For a moment, Bryan stood there and stared over their piles of equipment and belongings. "Okay, you've got your blankets and tent. Make sure to put your food in the bear box." He pointed to the large metal box sitting at the edge of camp. "If you want, I can help you get the tent set up."

"Dad-," Wyn started with a tone Lugh had never heard him use before.

"Okay, give your old man a break. This is the first time you've gone camping by yourself—further than the back yard." Bryan smiled. "I just feel like you're growing up. You've got a boyfriend, and you're going camping. In a few months, you'll even be driving." He walked over and ruffled Wyn's hair that was the same shade of blond as his own. "You're a good kid. I know you two will be fine, otherwise we wouldn't have agreed to this." He hugged Wyn and sighed. "You're almost taller than I am."

"Still got a few inches on me, Dad." Wyn stepped away from his father. "We'll be fine. Go on. If you take too long getting back, Mom'll worry about *you*."

Bryan nodded. "Yeah, she will." He walked over and hugged Lugh. At first, Bryan had struck Lugh as a little odd being so supportive, with hugs and wanted to be called by his first name, then Wyn told him that his dad was trying to fill in for Lugh's recently-passed father. Knowing that helped Lugh relax and accept him. Also being Wiccan, Wyn's family didn't have a lot of the same hang ups as most of the people Lugh knew, and they were okay with the boys dating as long as they stayed out of trouble.

"You two take care of each other the next couple of days." Bryan ruffled Lugh's red hair the way he had Wyn's. "I'll be back up here Monday afternoon. If you're not here at camp by three, I'll call Catherine, and she and the cats will be up here searching for you."

"If we're not here at three, I'll be screaming for Bast to come find us." Bran replied from the top of Lugh's backpack where he was walking around, kneading.

Lugh chuckled. "Bran says if we're not here then, he'll be calling Bast. So, Catherine'll know."

"Yeah, that's another good thing." Bryan said. For a moment it looked like he was going to try and find another reason to delay his departure, but he sighed, squared his broad shoulders and walked to the truck.

Lugh and Wyn stood side by side as he started the truck, waved and drove down the two-track that would take him back to the dirt road and on to highway 40 to Steamboat Springs. They stood there watching silently until the truck disappeared around a bend.

"Wow," Wyn said. "I thought he was never going to leave. He's not normally this over-protective."

"Hey, it's okay," Lugh replied. Since he'd lost his own father, he didn't mind Wyn's being over-protective. It wouldn't fill the void his father left, but it let him know there were others who cared about him. "At least he brought us up here and is letting us have this weekend to ourselves. I know a lot of kids whose parents wouldn't dream of letting them go camping alone."

Wyn smiled at Lugh. "They know we're not going to get into trouble."

Lugh nodded. "Yeah. And if we do, Bran can scream for help."

"*Of course I can.*" Bran looked up from the top of Lugh's backpack where he'd finally settled down. "*So are you going to set the tent up right away? I mean, just in case it starts raining.*"

Looking up into the cloudless blue sky, Lugh sighed in exasperation at his familiar. "It's not going to rain."

"If he's that worried about the rain from the clear sky, we can set up the tent," Wyn said. "Plus then, we can settle in and make out for a bit."

Lugh frowned. It wasn't that he didn't want to make out with Wyn, he thoroughly loved the time they spent being physically close, but he really loved hiking around in the new area he called home. "I thought we were going to go hiking. Not that I don't want to make out or anything, but we have time for that later… tonight… after the sun goes down."

Wyn laughed as he went and picked up the nylon bag with the tent inside. "Okay, we'll get the tent set up and the food stashed so we don't come back to bears eating our burgers." He glanced over at Bran. "So are you going hiking with us?"

"*I suppose I must, just in case something happens to my Magus,*" the cat replied. "*It wouldn't be right for me to let him get hurt or anything.*"

Lugh relayed the statement word for word. Bran had begun speaking to Wyn through Lugh. Abby thought it was funny, but Lugh's mom said it was something his father's golden retriever, Clarence, had done on occasion. It was apparently the way a familiar let their Magus know that they were accepting of the people or persons in their life. Like several other things about being a Magus, it was something Lugh was still getting used to.

Wyn chuckled as he pulled the tent out of the bag. "Don't worry, Bran, I don't want anything to happen to Lugh either."

Soon the two had the tent and camp set up, even though it meant disturbing Bran when Lugh carried his backpack into the small, green dome tent. Once they had everything set up to Wyn's discerning eye, they headed off down one of the three trailheads that started at the campsite.

3

Spark

"Do you think my chances of catching a hummingbird will be better if I just sit and wait for one to fly by?" Bran asked as they returned to camp after their hike. *"They make enough noise flying that they won't be able to sneak up on me."*

Lugh chuckled. "I don't have a lot of experience hunting hummingbirds, so I couldn't tell you."

Wyn looked at him and cocked an eyebrow.

"If I'm unsuccessful at grabbing one while we're camping, do you think we can talk your mother into putting up a feeder at the house? If we attract them, my chances of getting one goes up. They appear to be a most elusive prey. I bet even Matilda hasn't caught one." He'd been in awe of the hawk who was the familiar of one of the other Magi in the circle Lugh was part of. Although he stayed away from wild hawks, he was constantly asking Matilda for hunting advice.

"He's wanting to catch hummingbirds," Lugh relayed. "I bet Matilda hadn't bothered to try. It's probably safe to figure that they migrate south about this time of year." He glanced at Wyn for confirmation.

"Yeah." Wyn nodded as he walked toward the fire pit. "I'm actually surprised to see them now. It's been a warm year, so they are apparently delaying their departure. Some of the late-blooming flowers are still here. But they won't be around much longer."

"That may be good." Bran settled himself on a well-worn log next to the fire. *"In the spring I will be larger and faster. It'll improve my chances of catching one."*

"I don't think Mom'll be happy if you started bringing dead hummingbirds into the house." Lugh sat down next to Bran and scratched the cat's head. Having never had a kitten before, he'd been amazed how quickly Bran was growing from the small wet kitten he'd saved from the river into the sleek tom cat he was destined to be.

"Then I'll keep them outside. Lugh, you must let me grow into the accomplished hunter I'm destined to be. I don't try and inhibit your growth as a Magus."

"I guess not. We'll see what we can do."

Wyn walked over and stood in front of Lugh. "I hate to interrupt this very important conversation, but do you want to help me get the fire going?"

Lugh shrugged. "I guess I can. I thought you told your dad that you brought the fire starting kit."

"I did." Wyn frowned for a moment. "But I was thinking that once I got the wood ready, you could maybe practice making fire. Aren't you the one who's always telling me that you need to practice your magic as often as possible?"

"Yeah." Lugh nodded. He loved sharing his magic with Wyn. Having Wyn around and interested in magic was one of the things that made his transition from normal-every-day teenager to Magi easier. Wyn wanted to know everything he could about the magical forces Lugh tapped into and what made them different from the little folk magic Wyn and his family did in their Wiccan practices. "So get the wood set up and we'll do this. I guess this is a lot safer than practicing on paper in a metal garbage can on the back porch."

"As long as you don't set the forest on fire, we're great." Wyn flashed Lugh a smile as he carefully piled the wood in a cone shape toward the center of the fire ring. "We'll start small. I don't think we'll need a bonfire tonight."

"We'll need as much heat as possible to keep me warm." Bran licked his paws as he sat on the log next to Lugh.

"I'm pretty sure we don't need a bonfire to keep you warm," Lugh said.

Wyn looked over his shoulder at the cat. "You're wearing a fur coat. You can't be that cold."

Surprisingly Bran didn't respond but just kept licking his paws while his tail flicked in irritation.

After a moment, Wyn raised a blond eyebrow. "Well?"

Lugh shrugged. "No response. Kinda surprising after all."

"Bast has been reminding me that as a familiar and more importantly as a cat, I have a certain level of dignity to maintain."

A chuckle escaped Lugh. "Yeah." He smiled at Wyn. "He's claiming dignity."

"Okay fine, we'll go with that." Wyn placed another piece of wood into the cone shape and sat on the ground. He leaned against Lugh's legs.

An almost magical tingle still ran through Lugh whenever he and Wyn touched. He looked forward to the feeling whenever he'd gone any length of time without touching Wyn. Running his fingers through Wyn's hair, he couldn't help but smile. "So are you ready for me to do this?"

Wyn nodded. "Shoot. But explain to me what you're doing. I still think this might be something I can eventually figure out. It's not as complex as accessing the paths."

Lugh took a deep, steadying breath. He grounded himself the way he'd been taught. Each of the elements had its own magical frequency. Fire was higher than earth and water, but not as high as air.

"Let yourself relax," Lugh said. For a moment, he used a soft tone like Catherine used when she was teaching him.

Wyn took a deep breath.

"I'm reaching out for my ring, letting its energy open up so I amplify my perceptions. Fire exists all around us. Like the other elements, it's everywhere. I just have to tap into it. The spark is right here at my fingertips. I can see them glowing red as I find the frequency of fire." Lugh snapped his fingers and visualized a spark flying from them into the fire pit. "Watch the fire as it goes into the wood. Then all I have to do is see the logs burning." The spark blazed up, catching the dry tinder and their campfire was lit.

"That's just cool." Wyn laid his head on Lugh's knee. "I wonder if I found a ring, or even just a crystal that resonated with me, that I'd be able to focus energy like that. There are a lot of books out about the use of crystals in magic. I don't think it would be that hard, other than actually manifesting the flame.

One thing Dad said a while back, magic is like muscles, you have to exercise to get it in better shape."

Lugh nodded. "That sounds like something Catherine would say. She's all the time saying the more I practice, the stronger I'll be. There was something I overheard her saying to Henry, one of the other Magi, about she was surprised that Dad drowned. He'd mastered the elements when he was younger and he should've been able to use his magic to save himself."

"Did you ask her about that?"

"No, I didn't want her to know I'd overheard them. I was supposed to be helping Abby get the circle set up for ritual that night."

Wyn hugged Lugh's leg. "You never said if they found his body or not."

Lugh shook his head. "No, at least not that Mom has told me about. There was just the boat wreckage. But there's a few people every year that drown and they never find the bodies. The authorities just give up after a while."

"Do you think he might've used his magic to save himself?"

It was something he'd wondered ever since learning about magic. But he always came to the same conclusion. "Then why hasn't he found us? Tracking people by magic isn't too hard, unless they're trying to hide. You know, like the shield the dark Magi had up when they kidnapped you and Abby. Mom and I haven't been hiding here and it had been a few months after the accident when we left Florida. No, I don't think he's still alive. He'd be here if he was." Lugh swallowed hard. He would give anything for his father to be there with them. It would be so wonderful to be learning magic from him rather than Aunt Catherine. And if his father was still around, maybe his mother wouldn't be so sad all the time.

Wyn let go of Lugh's legs and raised himself onto the log. He wrapped his arms around Lugh's shoulders and kissed him. "Sorry, I didn't mean to make you sad. This is supposed to be a happy trip."

Lugh kissed him back. "I'm here with you, it is a happy trip."

"Look, before you two start with all the kissing and stuff, you could at least feed me." Bran pawed Lugh's leg and looked up with pitiful orange eyes. *"You haven't even set out any water I can get to. Starve yourselves, but don't starve me."*

Looking down at the cat, Lugh chuckled. "Okay. Fine. I'll feed you. Actually, I think I could use a bit of food myself." He rubbed Bran's head as he gave Wyn a parting kiss. "You said you'd cook this weekend. What's for dinner?"

"I was figuring burgers tonight, otherwise it's either hot dogs or cold cuts." Wyn got up and headed for the locked bear box where they'd secured their food.

Bran jumped off the log and followed. Instead of sitting there by himself, Lugh did the same. "Let's do hot dogs tonight. Lunch from school is still sitting heavy, so let's save the burgers for tomorrow night."

4

Glow in the Dark Girl

It was the first time Lugh had ever fallen asleep with Wyn next to him. They'd had a couple of sleepovers, but they hadn't actually slept in the same bed. With no parents around, they'd figured it was a good time to experiment a bit. They'd agreed to take things slow and they were. It was good, the little bit of playing around they did, but it felt odd with Wyn lying next to him even with Bran curled up on the pillow next to his head.

Lugh didn't move. He was comfortable. But he wondered what disturbed his sleep. Wyn's breathing was slow and steady. Bran purred softly in his slumber. He couldn't hear anything moving beyond the tent.

With a resolved sigh, Lugh carefully put his hands behind his head and tried to will himself back to sleep.

The minutes ticked by.

He tried the meditation techniques Catherine and Abby used. They always seemed to put him to sleep when he was practicing in the shop. With a deep breath he told himself to relax. After a couple of minutes, he acknowledged he was about as relaxed as he could get, but still his mind refused to go back to sleep.

His smoky quartz ring hummed on his finger. He let his mind merge with the energy of the ring. Lugh glanced around to see things through the ring's enhancement. In sleep, Wyn's aura was lighter than it normally was. A soft blue glow enshrouded him, small gold runners, like vines, reached from Wyn's aura toward Lugh. He'd seen them before and asked Catherine about them. She'd said it was a sign of Wyn's growing emotional attachment for Lugh. She'd explained that if he could see his own aura, he'd see little gold vines running toward Wyn. It was normal for people to show their attachments in their aura.

A strange light glowed outside the tent. For a moment, Lugh wondered if it wasn't someone walking through their camp with a flashlight. Then, he realized that there wasn't any noise associated with the light. He let his connection to his ring drop. The light vanished. When he reconnected with the ring, the light came back.

"Bran," Lugh bumped the cat, "what is that?"

"What is what?" Bran asked sleepily.

"What?" Wyn mumbled.

"That glow?" Lugh eased himself out of the sleeping bag. A magical tingle dance across him as he reached for the tent zipper.

"What glow?" Wyn asked. "I don't see a glow."

"I don't know what that is, Lugh. Do you really want to go outside with it?"

"It's something magical. I want to see what it is."

"*Then* I'd *better* go *with* you." Bran and Wyn managed to say in perfect unison that echoed strangely through Lugh's ears and head.

He stared at the two of them over his shoulder. If it hadn't been for him staying in synch with his ring and seeing their auras, he wouldn't have been able to make them out. "Don't ever do that again. That was just weird. Wyn, grab a flashlight. I can see using my magic and seeing auras." Lugh finished opening the tent.

As he stepped out of the tent, he looked to where he'd last seen the glow. It raced away into the trees. He was thankful he still had his jeans on, but the stones of the campsite bit into his sock-covered feet. Gritting his teeth, he ignored the pain and hurried after the fleeing glow. *That isn't just any glow, it's got to be someone.*

"Be careful, Lugh," Wyn called out behind him. "This forest can be dense and dangerous even in the daylight."

"I'm trying to be." Lugh stumbled over something that felt like a log. He barely caught his footing before he crashed into a standing tree whose aura glowed green in his magically enhanced sight.

"*Not very graceful tonight.*" Bran raced past him. "*Follow me! I can see the glow and the dead trees that don't have auras.*"

"So what is it?" Lugh followed the cat through the trees as the glow drew further away.

"*I don't know. I've never seen anything like it. The memories of my line don't have much on odd glows. I'd almost say it's a ghost, but it's not acting like any ghosts my ancestors have encountered.*" Bran had access to all the knowledge of the other familiars in his family tree. It was something that had come in handy before. Somehow knowing none of Bran's family had encountered such a glow made it a lot scarier.

"Does he know what it is?" Wyn asked from behind Lugh.

Lugh shook his head. "Nope, he says it looks like a ghost, but it's not acting like a ghost."

"Cool. So what does he mean that it's not acting like a ghost?"

"No clue." Since moving to Steamboat Springs and learning he had a magical family, Lugh had learned to not be irritated by things he didn't know. There was so much about his new life that had been alien to him when he first encountered it and at times it felt like the learning curve was going to be unending.

Ahead of them, the glow stopped fleeing. Lugh slowed his rush forward. The glow looked a lot more like a person now that it wasn't moving away from them. It looked like the back of a teenage girl.

"What are you?" Lugh called out.

Bran stopped a top of a fallen tree. *"I don't like this. It's never good when you're chasing something and it turns to fight."*

Lugh didn't reply. He watched at the glowing figure reached out its hand and made a motion. It looked like it was drawing a rune in the air, just like Lugh had been taught to so he could access the magical paths that Magi traveled. As a doorway onto the path opened up, something moved at the glowing girl's feet. A glowing dog vanished with her onto the path.

The door to the path closed and the glowing girl vanished.

5

Hiking

"Should we let Catherine know about the ghost girl?" Wyn asked the next morning as they sat eating their fruit and power bar breakfast.

Lugh yawned. They had talked about their encounter for a couple of hours until they fell asleep. His feet still hurt from running through the forest in his socks. "I don't think she meant us any harm. I wonder if she was drawn to me synching with my ring and looking at your aura while you slept."

Wyn cocked an eyebrow. "You were watching me sleep?"

"Something woke me up and I was trying to find something to relax me enough to go back to sleep." Lugh shrugged and stifled another yawn. "You're kinda cute when you're asleep, nice soft blue aura."

"Hey, I just emptied my bowl over here," Bran called from the tent.

"Be there in a minute," Lugh replied. "You're not going to starve before I get there."

"Is there any time that he's not hungry?" Wyn asked.

"When he's asleep."

"Did you watch him sleep too?"

Lugh nodded. "Yeah, he looked really peaceful before the glowing Magus girl showed up."

Wyn bit into an apple. "So, you're sure she was a Magus?"

"Even after sleeping on it, I'm pretty sure. She made a rune to access the air path that runs across the mountain. It's the path that goes across the continent. She also had a dog with her."

"Yeah, that was a familiar," Bran said. *"But ghosts don't have familiars."*

"Bran insists that ghosts don't have familiars." Lugh said, after he finished a section of orange. "Part of me wants to go tell Catherine about it and see what she has to say, the rest of me wants to figure it out on our own. At the very least, let's see what happens tonight. I want to try and trace her path through the forest, see if there is anything there we can spot that might help us."

"Do you think we can do that?" Wyn tossed his apple core into the cold remains of their fire.

"I got us back to camp last night," Bran replied. *"I can lead us along our trail through the forest."*

Lugh nodded. "Bran says he can lead us again. I wonder if I can see more in the daylight than I did at night."

"At least you won't be falling over logs and stuff." Wyn said, then smiled.

Lugh frowned, then chuckled. He was finding he couldn't be mad at Wyn for more than a minute or so. "I didn't realize that dead things don't have auras. It's a perfectly legitimate beginner's mistake. Hey, but I didn't fall."

Wyn shook his head. "No, but if I'd been able to get it on video, we might have won some big cash or at least your two minutes of fame on the internet. It was kinda funny after I got over the fear that you'd just fallen."

"Fine." Lugh tossed his orange peel at Wyn. "I'll remember that. Maybe when you're making that funny face you make when you're checking your teeth in the mirror."

Wyn laughed as he caught the orange peel and tossed it in the fire. "Okay, we'll wait until we do some more investigating before we alert Catherine. So how soon do you want to head out?"

"We're about done with breakfast-" Lugh started to say.

"Not all of us," Bran interrupted. *"My bowl went empty before I was done."*

"So after Bran has his fill," Lugh continued as if the cat hadn't butted in, "we can get on with it. Maybe afterwards we can do a bit of hiking and thinking."

"I can't see any more than I did last night." Lugh plopped down on the tree where Bran had stopped at the end of their pursuit of the glowing girl.

"You know, I've been thinking." Wyn sat beside Lugh as Bran prowled near the air path where the glowing girl disappeared. "I wonder if it might've been an astral projection as opposed to a ghost."

"An astral projection? What's that?"

"It where a person can separate their spirit from their body to go places their body can't or communicate with someone who's far away," Wyn explained.

"But that's why we have phones," Lugh replied.

"Astral projection has been around a lot longer than phones."

"He's right. But I don't think astral projections glow." Bran strolled beyond the point they had last seen the girl and looked around. *"Although, astral projection would explain the familiar showing up. It's not something that's easy to do. A Magus must be in perfect synthesis with their familiar to get it to work properly. It's not even something I think Catherine can do. If she can, it's not something Bast has shared with me."*

"But the glowing girl looked to be a teenager, like us," Lugh said. "Unless she is some kind of magical prodigy, how could she do it, and why would she come looking for us? It doesn't make any sense." As odd as a lot of it was, so far, most of the magical principle's he'd been taught made sense. It was one of the things Lugh liked about magic. But even if magic made sense, the people using it were still people and people did strange things.

"Did Bran just confirm that a Magus can use astral projection?" Wyn asked.

Lugh nodded. "But it's an advanced magic." He hadn't exactly figured out what constituted advanced magic over beginner stuff. A lot of times when he thought of something he'd thought would be cool, either Catherine or Abbey was quick to say it was advanced magic and they'd get around to it sometime in the future.

"So then we're back to her being a ghost?"

"Yeah."

"But there's nothing new to see here?"

Lugh watched Bran before answering. "Not that we can tell. If we knew a bit more, there might be something we could do, but as it stands right now, no."

"Then let's go on down the trail and get in a nice long hike," Wyn suggested. "That's why we're up here. We can see what happens tonight."

Lugh's breath caught. The trail before them opened up onto a vibrant green valley. Below them a large herd of elk strolled out of the trees and into the knee-high grass. For a minute, Lugh tried to count them, but there were too many moving around and he couldn't keep track of them all. Then a massive bull elk stepped out. His huge antlers swept back across his back, and he raised his muzzle up toward the clear blue sky. His shrill bugle rolled up from the valley. The other elk didn't respond, but the sound sent shivers through Lugh.

"Wow," he whispered, afraid to say anything too loud that might break the tableau unfolding below him.

"Yeah, it's really cool." Wyn said softly next to him. "I love it when I see stuff like this."

With the serenity of the scene broken, Lugh pulled out his cell phone and started snapping pictures. "This is so awesome." He kept his voice low and level. "I don't know which is more cool, seeing this, or seeing a blue whale while out boating."

Wyn smiled. "I think the blue whale would be, but then, I've never seen one. I've seen lots of elk, but they're still cool too."

Lugh nodded. He snapped a shot of the big bull chasing one of the small bulls off when it got too close to one of the cows. "I guess it all depends on where you're from and what you're used to. For me, dolphins racing along the bow of a boat is commonplace. When we saw the blue whale two years ago, that was the coolest thing I'd ever seen. But this, this is awesome. I've never seen anything like it. I wonder if the whole world was like this back when man was just coming out of the trees."

"As long as we don't have to go down there and risk me getting stepped on, I'm fine with it." Bran rolled over in the sunlit grass in front of Lugh's feet. *"I don't think I care to meet a whale or a dolphin. Unless they were willing to share fish with me. Then it might be interesting."*

Lugh chuckled as he kept taking pictures. He paused and looked at a few that he'd taken. In most of them, the elk were just large two-tone brown blobs on the screen. Frowning, he turned off the phone and slid it back in his pocket. "I need a real camera. It would be nice to get better pictures."

Wyn nodded. "Yeah, we have a small camera shop in town. A lot of the outdoor enthusiasts who come through need things from time to time, so they do a decent business. Mom and Dad are always sending folks over there. Dad's talking about getting this new small video camera that you can put almost anywhere, even on a hat. I've seen some of the video from them. Really cool. Something like that might be interesting for hiking. Most of what I've seen so far with it has been skiers and kayakers."

"I can see where that might be cool." Lugh watched as the lead bull pushed his cows away from the smaller bulls around the herd. "Dad used to take some really nice pictures, but he had his camera with him when the boat went down. They recovered that stuff, but it was ruined. If we had more money, I might be able to talk mom into buying me a camera for Christmas, but that'll probably have to wait." He paused. "Do you guys even celebrate Christmas?"

"Yes and no." Wyn shrugged. "We celebrate Yule, which is a few days before Christmas on the calendar and is a much older holiday. Some folks also call it Winter Solstice. We still give gifts, have a tree, lights and all that stuff."

Lugh smiled. "Good, Christmas always makes Mom happy. I'm hoping it'll help cheer her up this year, even if Dad's not around. It'll also be nice to buy you something cool."

"So what are you going to buy me?" Wyn asked.

For a second, Lugh looked away from the natural spectacle below them and smiled at Wyn. He loved looking into the other boy's intense blue eyes. "I don't know yet. But I want it to be cool."

"As long as we get to spend time together, that's what's important to me." Wyn leaned over and kissed Lugh.

Tingles shot through Lugh. "We'll definitely get to spend time together."

Bran rolled back to his feet, stretched and yawned. *"You know, I've already missed two naps this afternoon, not to mention, I'm thirsty. Are we heading back to camp any time soon? Because if we're not, but you guys are going to start making out, I can nap right here. As long as no clouds roll in, I'm fine in the sun here."*

Bending down, Lugh scooped the cat up in his arms and kissed the top of his head. "I think we missed lunch too, so unless Wyn thought to pack something, we should at least head back to get some food."

"I've got some energy bars, but a sandwich sounds better right now." Wyn shrugged. "If you guys want we can head back."

"Sure." Lugh looked back down into the valley as the elk were about to enter the trees on the far side. It didn't take them long to disappear into the forest. "This is just so awesome."

"Tomorrow, we can head the other way out of camp," Wyn said. "There are often some bighorn sheep on the eastern slope of the pass. But it will mean a bit more hiking."

Bran sighed as he jumped down from Lugh's arms. *"As long as you bring water, I suppose, if I get tired, I can ride on your backpack."*

6

Mistaken Identity

"How long do you want to sit up?" Wyn stood, yawned and put another log on the fire.

Lugh shrugged. "I don't know. What time is it?" He'd lost track of time after the sun disappeared over the western horizon. The lights of Steamboat Springs cast a bright glow silhouetting the mountains between their camp and the city.

"Eleven thirty." Wyn settled back in next to Lugh on the log in front of the tent.

"I don't remember what time she showed up last night." Lugh looked over at Bran, curled up asleep, as close to the fire as he could comfortably get. "If she is some kind of ghost, shouldn't she be stuck on a schedule or something?"

Now it was Wyn's turn to shrug. "Don't know much about ghosts. They say there are several in the old buildings down town. Most of them are memory imprints that just repeat the same actions day and day. Those are the kinds that are on schedules. I can't say as anyone has ever reported a ghost being up here before. Or at least not one that I've heard about."

"And I'm asleep, so don't ask me," Bran added, without opening his eyes. *"I've already told you everything I, and my ancestors, know."*

Not for the first time during their camping trip, Wyn was tempted to call Catherine and ask her opinion on the glow. But, he was enjoying the time alone with Wyn so much that he wanted to wait as long as he could before involving anyone else in the situation.

"I'm working on tired, but let's give it a little while longer." Lugh glanced at the log that was starting to catch fire. "Let's give it until the log burns down." He put his arm over Wyn's shoulder and pulled him close. "Nobody's going to catch us this late. Let's keep enjoying the moonlight for a while longer."

Wyn smiled. "Are you determined to wear my lips off this weekend?"

"Maybe." Lugh chuckled as they kissed again. Wyn was such a good kisser; he was determined not to let opportunities pass them by.

A dull orange glow, softer than Bran's eyes, lingered in the fire pit. Lugh accepted Wyn's hand up from the ground. Without Wyn's arms around him, the chilly wind brushed across him, tearing through his thin t-shirt. They'd brought jackets, but with the fire, they hadn't needed them until they started moving around.

"Log's done, let's hit the bed," Wyn said. "We'll give her another opportunity tomorrow night." He yawned. "But right now, I need some sleep."

"Me too." Bran stretched and yawned as he walked toward the tent. *"You do remember that I missed naps this afternoon?"*

Lugh looked around, scanning the dark forest, hoping for some sign of the strange blue glow he'd seen the previous night. But other than the city glow, nothing caught his attention. "Okay, let's get some sleep so we can go try and find the big horn sheep tomorrow."

"Sounds good." Wyn hit the button on the flashlight and walked over to the tent.

"He can't even find the zipper in the moonlight," Bran said.

"The light helps me too," Lugh replied.

"Is he complaining about the flashlight?" Wyn turned the light on the cat. Bran paused looked up at him and hissed.

Lugh chuckled. "I think that answers your question."

Wyn frowned at Bran. "You know, not all of us are gifted with super night vision." He opened the tent and stepped in. "But I've got thumbs and you don't."

Bran bounced in without a reply.

Even after Wyn and Bran were asleep, Lugh still tossed and turned. In his mind, he kept seeing the blue glow and wondered what it was exactly and why it was there.

"Colin?" a soft voice called from outside the tent.

Lugh opened his eyes. He synched his mind with his ring and magic hummed around him. The glow was back. He lay there for a moment. Beside him, Wyn breathed slowly and steadily. Bran purred in his sleep, inches above Lugh's head and the strange blue glow filled the tent with an eerie light.

Although part of him wanted to wake his boyfriend and the cat, he thought better of it. *Maybe all three of us together is what scared her away last night.*

"Colin?" the voice repeated.

The last dregs of sleepiness flew away as the name sank in. Colin had been his father. Lugh slid out of the sleeping bag, trying desperately not to wake Wyn. He had to get outside and see who or what the glowing girl was.

To his relief, the zipper opened quietly. He stepped out into the chilly night and spotted the blue ghostly girl standing near the fire pit. Her long hair looked strawberry blonde, even through the blue aura that enshrouded her. Her bell-bottom jeans were out of fashion, as was her white blouse with its billowy cuffs. At her side stood a red cocker spaniel that glowed with same not-quite-neon blue.

"What are you?" Lugh didn't bother closing the tent flap. If something went wrong, Bran could get to him easier. "Who are you?"

"Don't you remember me, Colin?" The glowing girl frowned. "It's me, Espe."

"I think you have me confused with my father." Lugh walked over so the fire pit was between them.

"Colin McNeal is your father?" Espe's face fell. The cocker spaniel pushed against her leg and looked up at her. "But Colin said he'd wait for me. He can't be your father. He's just sixteen." She stared at Lugh. Some form of magic flowed out of her. It sent shivers through Lugh.

"Lugh are you alright?" Bran shouted from the tent.

"Ouch!" Wyn shouted. "Bran get off me! Where's Lugh!"

Espe and her familiar turned and ran from the campsite.

"Espe, come back!" Lugh shouted. He crashed over the log he and Wyn had spent the evening sitting on. His face hit the cold ground really hard. Stars flashed in his vision.

"*Lugh!*" Bran and Wyn yelled, again in perfect stereo.

"I told you two not to do that again." Lugh rolled over and sat upright before Bran hit him in the chest. "My head hurts enough without you two yelling at me in stereo."

"*Why were you out of the tent without us?*" Bran looked at him while standing in his lap with front paws on his chest.

"The blue glowing girl was back." Lugh rubbed his nose. It was sore, but he didn't think it was broken. "Her name is Espe. She thought I was Dad."

"You actually talked to her this time?" Wyn sat down on the ground next to Lugh.

Lugh nodded and pain lanced through his face where he'd hit the ground. "Yeah. I didn't get much. She did something with magic. She must've woken up Bran. When you two started shouting she and her cocker spaniel ran. I tripped over the log and they got away. I think whatever I did let her know I wasn't Dad."

"So she's a Magus of some sort," Wyn said.

"*But none of my line has ever heard of a blue glowing Magus before,*" Bran settled down into Lugh's lap. "*We've got to consult Catherine on this.*"

"Bran wants us to consult Catherine on it," Lugh relayed. "It's too late to call tonight. We could wait until morning."

In the soft light of the half moon, Wyn frowned. "What do you wanna bet that they want us to come home after we call?"

Lugh let out a sigh of regret. "Probably. But something tells me this might be important. If it's something that none of Bran's lineage has ever encountered, she might be more than we can deal with. Plus, something about the way she ran off this time makes me think she might need help."

"Why do I get the feeling you're about to say we have to help her?" Bran glared up at Lugh.

"Well if she needs help then we have to do what we can," Wyn said. "I've never helped in any magical way."

"I was wrong, he said it."

Lugh smiled at Wyn and looked out into the forest, in the direction Espe had disappeared. As the pain in his head cleared, the idea that she needed their help solidified. Even if Bran complained about it, he wanted to do what he could to help her. *She thought I was Dad. Is she an old friend of his?* There was no way he wasn't going to try to help.

7

Omissions Old and New

Lugh shifted uneasily under the watchful eyes of his mother, Catherine, and Wyn's parents. Just a few minutes after his call to Catherine, she along with Bast arrived at their camp, using the same air path to get up the mountain that Espe had disappeared into the first night. About an hour later Wyn's father came up, helped them pack up camp and hauled the boys, and cats along with Catherine, back to Steamboat Springs.

They all sat in Lugh's living room as he, Wyn and Bran recounted what happened.

"And you're sure she said her name was Espe?" Catherine asked. Bast sat in her lap and she'd been rapidly petting the cat. In the short time Lugh'd known her, he'd come to realize that this was a nervous habit for her. He'd only seen her do it a few times.

Lugh nodded. "She didn't give her last name, but her first name was definitely Espe. I'm also sure her familiar was a cocker spaniel."

"Does this mean anything?" Lugh's mother asked.

Catherine nodded. "Unfortunately it does, Margaret. Espe Colman disappeared about twenty-five years ago. I'll have to check with mother to be sure exactly when, but she and Colin had been dating before the two of you got together." She sighed as she continued to stroke Bast. "Colin was really broken up when she disappeared. I remember everybody saying that she hadn't been trained correctly and something had happened to her on the paths. Those of us in training at the time didn't believe them. We were sure something else caused her disappearance. She had more promise than any of us at the time. I honestly think she scared some of the older Magi with the quickness that she picked things up. Her disappearance devastated Colin." For a moment Catherine's gaze rested on Lugh's mom, then she shook her head. "After that, he swore he'd never get involved with another Magus again. He didn't want to risk losing someone again without knowing what happened to them. I think Espe's disappearance gave him the strength to walk away from magic as easily as he did."

"I never knew," Lugh's mother whispered.

"But your family is from Colorado Springs," Bryan Chambers said. "How did her ghost get all the way to Rabbit Ears Pass?"

Catherine shrugged. "I don't know. There's not a lot of evidence of Magi ghosts. I've heard of spirit guides who appear in times of need. But this doesn't sound like that."

"What's a spirit guide?" Lugh asked. Other than answering questions, he'd been fairly quiet since getting home, absorbing the information that was being offered by the adults talking.

He'd actually been fairly surprised about how quiet Abby was being. His cousin normally had an opinion on everything.

"A spirit guide, as far as Magi are concerned, are the spirits of Magi that haven't reincarnated yet. They show up with knowledge we might not be able to get any other way. There haven't been any documented cases of them appearing here in the states in over a hundred years. There were one or two in England during the second world war, but not since."

"And if she's a spirit guide, why did she appear to Lugh at this time?" Stephanie Chambers, Wyn's mother asked.

"No clue." Catherine shot another glance at Lugh's mom, and sighed. "It's been a few months since we've had any activity out of the Dark Magi."

"Wait a minute!" Lugh's mother straightened in her chair and glared at Catherine. "Dark Magi? Nobody said anything about there being Dark Magi. Colin never mentioned it and you didn't until now. What in the hell is a Dark Magus?"

Lugh cringed. He knew his mother cussed from time to time, but when she did it in a room full of people she was getting pissed off. He hoped this wasn't going to get nasty. There were more than a few times when she'd get mad and threaten to move away from Steamboat and take him somewhere safe.

Catherine stroked Bast hard enough that the cat glared at her before jumping off the couch and sitting at her feet. "Margaret, I didn't want to worry you. You've had enough to deal with since Colin's passing. I figured it would go better if you didn't know."

"If I didn't know that my son was in danger?" His mother's voice took on a dangerous tone.

"Wow, the way they're growing, they're about to tear out fur," Bran said from Lugh's lap.

Lugh ignored the cat. He reached across the space between his and his mother's chairs and took her hand. "Mom, I'll be fine. Catherine is a great teacher and I'm learning fast. We don't need to worry about the Shadow Magi doing anything to us."

"If it helps, we trust Catherine," Bryan said. "She's a pillar of the magical community here in Steamboat."

His mom smiled at the Chambers. "Bryan, Stephanie, I appreciate you're backing Catherine in this. I understand. But it's my understanding that Magi magic is a bit more complex than Wiccan magic. That in itself makes it more dangerous. Now I find out that are dark shadow Magi out there." She looked at Lugh. "Why did you just call them Shadow Magi when Catherine has been calling them dark Magi?"

"You know, I think I'm going to go get a drink of water." Bran jumped off Lugh's lap and headed for the kitchen. *"It might be safer in another room."* The other cats in the room followed him out.

Lugh gulped. "Because that's what they call themselves. I met a couple right after I got my ring. But we don't know if they have anything to do with Espe."

"Are you trying to change the subject, young man?" his mother asked.

"Actually, I think he's trying to get us back on track." Wyn spoke for the first time in several minutes. "We're supposed to be trying to figure out what's going on with Espe. The Shadow

Magi were taken care of months ago." He shot a glance at his parents who had both gotten still with very concerned looks on their faces.

Lugh's mother fixed her gaze on Catherine. "We'll talk about the Dark or Shadow Magi …whatever you call them…later."

Catherine nodded but remained silent.

"So how do we find out about what happened to Espe?" Lugh asked.

"I can contact her family," Catherine said. "I think they still live outside Colorado Springs. There's a possibility that if she has come back as a ghost, she may have visited them first. They might also remember something about what happened to her back then that they didn't want to let me know when it happened. It's possible they were afraid to scare us."

"I don't know, from the sound of it, Magi are pretty good about not telling everyone everything in an attempt to keep them safe." Lugh's mom squeezed his hand a little tighter than she needed to, but he didn't say anything about it.

"So what can we do while you look into this?" Stephanie asked. "I realize this is a Magi thing, but we do know a little bit about ghosts. There's a good possibility we can use some of the more down to earth magics to at least contact her and find out why she's here, now."

"That might not be a bad idea," Catherine said. "I can chase down some background information through Magi sources while you see what you can find out through traditional magical means."

"So where does that leave us?" Lugh asked. From the look on Wyn's face, he was about to ask a similar question.

"She's coming to you." Stephanie looked at Lugh. "Even if she did think you were your father, she's making a connection. We can use that to reach out to her."

"I want to help with this," Wyn said. "I was there too."

Stephanie reached out and patted her son's knee. "I think we can let you help, Abby, too, if she wants to."

Abby perked up. "Oh yeah, anything you need. I'm your girl." Then she looked at her mother. "If it's okay with Mom."

Catherine nodded. "It's Wiccan magic, I don't think there'll be any harm in it, even if you are dealing with a Magus spirit and her familiar."

"I wonder if we could work out a way for our familiars to speak to hers?" Lugh's mind began churning with excitement. He was going to get to learn more about Wiccan magic. Even if it was supposed to be weaker than Magus magic, it was still another form of magic and he wanted to know as much about it as he could.

Bryan Chambers looked thoughtful for a moment. "That's something you and the familiars will need to work out. Until Wyn and Catherine came and told us about you all, the Magus were just legends to us. We don't really know how the whole familiar bond works when it comes to the magics involved. But we're willing to try. With Samhain just a week away, the veil between the living world and the spirit world is growing thinner. It'll be the perfect time to work on this."

Lugh smiled to himself. This had a lot of potential to be really interesting. He'd already met a ghost, now they were going to figure out how to summon her so they should find out what she can and discover a way to help her. With what Catherine said, he knew for sure she needed help.

8

The Wrath of Mom

After everyone had left, Lugh's mom closed the door, leaned against it with her arms crossed and glared at him. It was a look he'd seen before and one he'd hoped to avoid whenever possible.

"So, when were you going to get around to telling me about the Shadow Magi?" Her voice was disturbingly soft and even.

Lugh gulped. "I would've gotten around to it eventually."

"Eventually?" She shoved herself off the door and stalked toward him. "I believe one of the conditions I gave to both you and Catherine when I agreed to let her teach you magic was that I was to be kept abreast about everything that was going on. Did these Shadow Magi have something to do with the kittens who were killed about the time you bonded to Bran?"

Bran walked into the hall at the same time she said his name. *"You know, I think I'm going to go curl up in the pool of sunshine on your bed. It still doesn't feel safe in here."*

"Yes." Lugh nodded, again not acknowledging his familiar. "They were behind it."

"Were you ever in any danger?" Her stance grew harsher

"A bit." He knew he had to tell the truth, anything else and she'd get so upset she'd move them away from Steamboat Springs and he'd never see Catherine, Abby, or Wyn again.

"How much?"

"I don't really know." Lugh leaned against the doorframe going into the living room. It felt supportive, but at the same time, he couldn't back up any farther. "They'd kidnapped Abby and Wyn. Bran and I found them and managed to rescue them."

"Wait a minute." A look of dawning crossed her face and she ran a hand through her brown hair. "Was that the child molester case two months ago? The guy who'd picked up some poor girl on the street?"

Lugh nodded again. "That was it. Catherine worked some kind of magic on the cops to keep Wyn and me out of the picture. Abby was the only one the police think was involved."

Her face grew dangerously hard and she squinted at him. "And whose idea was it to keep me in the dark about this? Do the Chambers know about it?"

"I asked Catherine not to tell you about it." Lugh actually felt a little better admitting the truth. He didn't want his mother getting mad at his aunt for something he'd asked her to do. "I was afraid you might get stressed out over it and stop me from my Magi training. Mom, it's so important to me. I don't want to do anything that's going to stop me from learning."

"You've never lied to me before." She pursed her lips and frowned. "Of course, I guess you didn't exactly lie to me, you just didn't tell me everything. Maybe we need to rework our agreement."

For a second, Lugh's heart sank into his stomach. A feeling of dread settled over him as his mother leaned against the doorframe on the opposite side of the door from him.

"From now on, you are to tell me everything that happens. I mean *everything*. I don't care if it's magical or not. Each night, over dinner or before bed, we're going to sit down and talk about what happened in your day. I may not be a Magus, but I'm your mother, I think I can tell when you're lying. If you want to keep studying magic," — she paused and glared at him — "or for that matter, if you want to keep dating, you're going to be honest with me. I'll compare notes with Catherine as to what's going on. If there are any discrepancies, we'll be talking about it. Depending on how far off things are, I'll determine what the punishment will be."

There was logic to what she was telling him. She wasn't really asking for his buy in. By her stance and tone, Lugh knew there wasn't going to be any negotiation on this new regulation. He could only hope that after a few months of total transparency, maybe she'd lighten up a bit. At least she wasn't shouting or crying, and she wasn't telling him he had to stop studying magic or seeing Wyn. Either one was more than he wanted to contemplate giving up.

"We can do that."

His mother nodded. "Yeah, I think *we* can. It might not be a bad idea if Wyn and his folks come to a similar agreement. That way we'll all know what's going on all the time. I don't know if you realize how much trust we're giving you boys right now. We had a really long talk about letting the two of you go camping before we agreed to it. You've both got it really good with parents who are as understanding as we are."

"Yeah, I think we do realize." For a moment, Lugh hoped the slight change in subject, away from magic and onto dating was a good sign. She hadn't relaxed any that he could tell, but the air in the doorway seemed to be getting lighter.

"Then just don't make us regret being understanding, in anything. As long as you're upfront and honest about *everything* that's going on, things'll keep on the way they've been. But don't think I'm not paying a lot more attention now." She sighed and reached out to take him in her arms.

With the hug, Lugh knew the worst of his mother's anger was passing, at least in that moment.

As she released him, she held him at arm's length. "I just don't want anything to happen to you. Your father hasn't even been gone a year, I couldn't stand losing you right now."

"Mom, you're never going to lose me. I'm going to be right here for you, forever."

She smiled and shook her head. "And don't make promises you can't keep. Besides, I want you to go off to college one of these days, after high school. You'll be gone then. And what happens when you find that man of your dreams, if you haven't already, and want to move in together?"

"I'll still be around. We've got each other, Mom."

"*And me.*" Bran appeared in the hallway.

Lugh chuckled. "And we've got Bran."

His mother looked down at the gray cat and smiled a tight sad smile. "And we've got Bran." She squatted down on the floor and scratched his head. "At least he'll do what he can to keep you out of trouble."

"That's one of the goals of every familiar, to protect their Magus." Bran leaned against her hand and purred loudly. It made Lugh feel good that his mother was at least getting comfortable enough with Bran to pet him. It gave him hope that she'd relax more about his magic as time went on.

A. M. Burns

9

Minding the Store

When the phone rang the next morning during breakfast, Lugh's mother got it before he could even start to get out of his chair. She was quiet for a moment, then nodded. "I think the responsibility will do him some good. I'll let you ask him." She handed the phone to Lugh. "It's your Aunt Catherine."

"Morning, Catherine," Lugh said, after swallowing a bit of waffle quickly.

"Lugh," she sounded worried. "I have a favor to ask of you."

He set his fork down and looked across the table at his mother. He couldn't tell anything from her neutral expression. "Sure, what do you need?"

"I've got to go out of town today. I need you to help Abby and Wyn mind the store for me."

With her worried tone and the fact that she hadn't mentioned anything about needing his help the previous day when they'd come home early, a stab of fear went through him. "Sure. Is anything wrong?"

"I don't know yet. I'll explain more when you get here. If your mom doesn't mind driving you over, that would be great. I need to get on the road."

Lugh looked at his mom who just nodded slightly like she already knew what was going on. "We'll be there in a few minutes."

"Thanks." And Aunt Catherine was gone from the line.

"You're okay with this?" Lugh asked as he picked up his fork to finish his breakfast as fast as he could.

"Sure." His mother put the phone back on the charger. "You're too young for a regular job, but I think the responsibility of the shop for a few hours will do you some good."

"Wyn says next summer we can probably work at his folks' place." Lugh had been wishing for a way to help his mother with the tight finances and getting a summer job would definitely be a step in the right direction.

She smiled and carried her own plate to the sink. "We'll talk about that more next year after your birthday. Now, finish up your breakfast and let's get going. Your aunt has a long day ahead of her."

"Bran!" Lugh shouted between bites.

"What? I'm sunning in the living room. It's really nice and warm. After you trying to freeze me on the mountain, I deserve a little warm sunshine."

"We've got to get going. Go find your harness and leash and we can go." Lugh finished up his waffle and headed toward the sink with his plate.

"You know I'm not a dog," Bran replied.

"Dear, he's not a dog," his mother said at the same time.

Lugh shook his head, not wanting to think about what it meant if Bran and his mother were going to start thinking the same. "I know, but he's done it before. When *he* wants to go somewhere." He ran a short blast of water into his plate, just enough the syrup wouldn't be so hard to get off when he got home and had to do the dishes.

"And who says I want to go this time?" Bran appeared in the kitchen with his harness and leash in his mouth. They were both thin enough for the half-grown kitten to carry easily.

"We're going to the shop." Lugh scooped up Bran and his accessories while heading toward the front door where his shoes waited on the mat his mother put there so he wouldn't track mud into the house.

"Why?" Bran squirmed in Lugh's arms.

"We're going to help Abby and Wyn man the place today. It's going to be fun." As Lugh reached his shoes, he'd realized he'd forgotten to ask Aunt Catherine if he was going to get paid.

"I can't officially pay you," Catherine said as she gathered her coat and purse. "But you three will get some money for helping out."

"Cool!" Lugh loved the idea of being able to earn a little bit of money.

"Abby understands how to operate the register and the credit card machine." Catherine put on her coat. "I'd close for the day, but with it being less than a week until Samhain, there's going to be lots of regulars in to get supplies. You three should know where everything is, you spend enough time in here."

"We'll do fine, Catherine," Wyn said before Lugh could.

"Good. Abby, it's okay to tell them what's going on." She stepped through the beaded curtain into the back room. "I'm hoping this is all for nothing, but it might not be." Bast appeared at Catherine's side, then the two of them hurried out the back door.

"And if you need anything, just call," Lugh's mother said as she headed for the front door. "I'll come by in a couple hours and bring you kids some lunch." Then she was gone too.

Lugh looked at Abby. He'd expected to get an explanation of what was going on from Aunt Catherine when he got to the store, but she'd been in such a hurry to leave, she hadn't said much beyond basic instructions. "So what's up?"

"She can't get a hold of Espe's family. She's going to Colorado Springs to look for them," Abby explained as she settled herself on the stool behind the cash register.

"Is that really a reason to drive all that way?" Wyn asked. "I mean, she is driving and not taking the paths."

Lugh looked toward the back of the shop. He hadn't felt his aunt use magic to access the paths, and had thought he'd heard her Jeep start up. "I didn't feel her use magic."

"It's easier sometimes to use mundane methods," Abby explained. "Depending on where you're going, unless you want to do a lot of walking after you get there, it's just easier to take a car; that way you can get around without appearing and disappearing around people."

"Okay, but that's like four hours one way," Wyn said.

On their way to Steamboat Springs, Lugh remembered driving through Colorado Springs which had seemed a bit like a southern suburb of Denver even with the few minutes of open space between the two areas. He didn't remember much about the time it had taken them to get from one place to another. The land had been so different from anything he'd been exposed to before that it had held his attention and he hadn't been aware of the passage of time. "So she's going to be gone all day."

"Right. She's lucky we aren't in school today. Sometimes things happen for a reason." Abby moved a couple of things on the counter in front of her stool. "Stella called in sick on Friday. Mom checked with her, but she's still under the weather. I think this is the perfect time for us to show Mom we can handle things while she's gone. I mean, I can't do readings, or anything like that, but the rest of it will be a snap."

Lugh was suddenly wishing Catherine's part time helper, Stella, had been available. He hadn't thought about people coming in for tarot card readings. It was one of the services Catherine provided that he had no idea how to do. She'd showed him the cards a couple of times, but the idea of the symbols meaning different things when they were laid out in different orders was very confusing to him. She hadn't pushed for him to learn it just yet and kept saying it was something that would come to him over time. He really hoped they wouldn't have anyone come in for a reading while Catherine was out. It would feel like he was disappointing her if a customer came in with a need they couldn't fulfill.

"We'll do fine," Wyn said.

The front door opened and a pair of customers walked in.

"Hey, I know these folks," Wyn added. "See, this is going to be easy and fun."

Lugh didn't want to mention how quickly words like that tended to be thrown back on the person who had uttered them. He suddenly wished he could go into the back room and curl up with Bran and Morrigan and take a nap. It would probably be a lot safer than trying to help take care of the shop.

10

The Secretive Shopper

During the morning, they only had a few shoppers come in. Most of them were regulars who were surprised to see Abby and Wyn manning the store. They all knew what they wanted and where it was, so Lugh, Wyn and Abby didn't have much to do except weigh out herbs, make change and wrap a couple of ceramic statues they couldn't find the original boxes for. By the time his mother came back with their lunch, he was fairly sure he could do just about anything in the shop, beyond readings.

It was being a fairly easy day, but when he took his hamburger into the back room to eat it quickly, he was surprised how much his legs complained. He wasn't used to standing around so much.

"Are you going to eat all of that?" Bran asked, jumping from the shelf where the cat bed was.

"My mom brought it for me." Lugh looked down at Bran as the cat stretched twice before sauntering over to him. "There's always kibble out for you guys."

Bran jumped up on the small table Lugh was eating at. *"Kibble…Really? Your mom always gets me the good stuff. Come on, you could give me a piece. I can haz cheese burger."*

"I think my mom is soft on you. She's spoiling you." The way his mother had acted when his Magus powers had first shown up and he'd bonded with Bran, that was something he never would've dreamed of saying. "Most cats survive on kibble."

"No." Bran stalked over to Lugh, then sat and stared at him. *"Most cats survive on mice and small birds. I'm not supposed to do that either. At least I get canned food. Although if you'd please tell your mom that the turkey and giblets is a lot better than the chicken and split pea, I'd appreciate it. Ever since you told me they make vomit in the movies out of split pea soup, I just can't eat that stuff anymore."*

Lugh sighed and tore off a small piece of his burger, making sure to get a little cheese on it before setting it on the table for Bran. "Okay, you win. Have a piece and I'll talk to mom."

Bran quickly ate the food, then wiped a paw across his whiskers. *"Thank you."*

Once Lugh was finished with his lunch, he headed back into the front of the store. Abby was still on the stool, and Wyn was helping a woman with some herbs.

"Did I miss anything?" Lugh leaned up against the counter by the cash register.

Morrigan was sprawled there and looked at him before laying her head back on her paws. It seemed odd that Bast wasn't there. But Bast had gone with Catherine. Lugh wished they would hear something from his aunt.

Abby shook her head. "Nothing unusual or different from this morning. Morrigan says you're spoiling Bran. Too much human food and he'll never be a good hunter."

"I will too!" Bran shouted as he slid through the beaded curtain. *"She's just jealous! Abby didn't share with her."* He glared at Morrigan as he hoped up on the counter

Lugh rolled his eyes and didn't bother replying to his familiar.

The bell on the door opened and a young Goth-looking woman walked in. She was tall, pale and dressed in black. She stopped a few feet into the store and looked at the candles in the display there. An odd energy emanated from her.

"There's something odd about her," Bran said, confirming the strange feeling Lugh felt when he looked at her.

Lugh wanted to stay behind the counter with Abby, but Wyn was busy, and Aunt Catherine prided herself of making sure every customer was welcomed into the store. He forced himself to walk over to her. "Hi, can I help you find anything?"

She shook her head. "Just looking." She glanced up at the counter. "You know, I've never seen the gray cat before. Isn't there normally a different cat here?"

Lugh reflexively looked at the counter where Bran and Morrigan were on separate corners. Her observation told him she was normally in the shop on the weekends since during the week when he was at school, Bran was there with Morrigan and Bast. "He's my cat."

"Oh." The woman turned back to the candles. "I'll let you know if I need anything."

Understanding he was being dismissed, Lugh returned to the counter just as Wyn escorted his customer over with an armful of little bags containing herbs. He read off the names and prices so Abby could put them into the cash register and moments later that woman had her bag and was heading out the door.

"Wow, that was our best sale of the day," Abby said. "A few more like that and Mom might decide to leave it in our hands all the time."

Lugh rolled his eyes and shook his head. "I hope not. We've still got school." He wasn't ready to drop out of school and work in the shop all the time. It was interesting, but not that much fun.

"Right," Wyn said. "Although alternating between here and my folks' shop this summer might be a lot of fun."

"It might," Abby agreed.

"She's doing something!" Bran shouted as a strange tingle of magic hit Lugh. At the same time, Abby and Wyn stopped and stared at the young woman standing by the candles. She hadn't moved more than a couple of steps since Lugh had talked to her.

As if she felt all their attention on her, the woman held up a hand and smiled. "Sorry, just trying to get a feel for the area."

Lugh wanted to ask her what she was trying to feel, but opted not to.

"Don't worry about it," Abby said before Lugh could find the right words.

"Well, you three have a good day." She waved, then walked out of the shop.

"What was she just doing?" Wyn asked. "It was something. I felt it."

Abby frowned and looked at Morrigan. "We're not sure."

"Bran?" Lugh stared at the cat.

"She was looking for something, or trying to get a feel for something." Bran shook his head. *"I don't really know."*

After dealing with the Shadow Magi right after bonding with Bran, Lugh didn't like the unknown, particularly not when it came in the guise of strange people coming into the shop. He really wished Aunt Catherine would come back so they could tell her what just happened. Maybe if she'd been there, the strange Goth woman wouldn't have done whatever it was she'd done to set them all off. But it was powerful enough for Wyn to feel it. That worried Lugh, unless what she'd done had been Wiccan Earth Magic, the type Wyn was more aligned to. That would explain it, but if it had been that, why had the cats reacted so badly to it?

Wyn's father, Bryan, showed up a few minutes after the strange woman left. "How's it going, you three?"

"Well," Wyn glanced at Lugh and Abby as if asking for permission to tell him about their strange customer.

Lugh gave him a quick nod.

"There was an odd customer a couple of minutes ago," Wyn continued.

Bryan raised an eyebrow. "Odd how?"

Lugh stood next to Wyn. "She didn't really want to talk to us, she just studied the candles, and asked questions about the cats."

"Studied the candles how?" Bryan didn't sound convinced there was a problem with the woman. "A lot of purists will only use beeswax candles; extremely white witches especially won't use anything made with oil-based products since they feel that the oil used to be dinosaurs and might mar their magic by being construed as a sacrifice."

"That's crazy." Lugh hadn't heard that from Aunt Catherine, then reminded himself that she wasn't teaching him wiccan magic, but a form of high magic that was a very different thing.

"Crazy or not, some people feel that way." Bryan frowned and glanced at Abby.

Abby shook her head. "The boys are totally missing the point here. It doesn't matter that she was studying the candles or asking about the cats. She did some kind of scanning magic. It's like she was searching for something. The cats felt it."

Bryan's frown deepened. "Scanning magic. Yeah. Okay. We have a potential problem." He pulled out his phone. "We'll get something done about this."

Lugh wondered what he was talking about as he hit a couple of buttons, then turned his back to talk.

Wyn smiled. "Wow, Dad's calling in reinforcements."

11

A Watchful Coven

Members of the Chambers' coven showed up in the shop a few minutes after Brian started calling them. Lugh hadn't met many of them, although a few of them showed up at Wyn's place above the outdoors shop from time to time, or came to the open circles Catherine held at the shop on full moons and holidays.

"Thanks for coming quickly," Bryan called them together after three of them were there. "Like I told you on the phone, Catherine was called out of town and Stella's laid up right now. The kids are handling things pretty well, but they had a strange customer a little while ago and I want us to stay handy until the shop closes."

One lady, who appeared to be the same age as Lugh's mother, looked from Lugh, to Wyn and Abby. "You guys are just starting out, aren't you?"

Abby frowned at her, but didn't say anything.

"Lugh is," Wyn replied. "But you've known Abby for years, Shelia."

She combed her fingers through her long black hair, then frowned slightly at some of the gray there. "I know. Sorry. Sometimes I'm not as articulate as I'd like. Of course Abby isn't just starting out. But the magic of adults is a little different from children's magic, isn't it?"

Bryan touched her arm. "So, Shelia, what we're needing is to make sure the kids are alright, especially if that customer comes back. She was a younger Goth woman. She appeared to have some magic at her disposal. I don't honestly think anyone will do anything with all of us here, but I want to make sure."

"Of course, Bryan." Shelia gestured to the others. "We'll just sit over at the table where Catherine does her readings and be here if you need us."

"That's all I was looking for," Bryan replied. He glanced at Lugh, Wyn and Abby. "We'll stay out of the way. I just want to make sure everything's okay. Catherine is the one who normally deals with strange magic in Steamboat, but she's out of town."

Wyn nodded. "We understand, Dad. Don't worry about being a father."

Bryan grinned and hugged Wyn. "You know, it's not very often I get to be over protective of you. It feels good."

A customer came in, and Bryan went over to sit with his coven mates. After that, several more customers came in and Lugh kind of lost track of things until Abby slammed the cash register a little harder than she needed to.

Lugh waited until the customer left and he looked at Abby. "Hey, what's wrong?"

Abby frowned and crossed her arms but didn't say anything.

After thinking about it for a moment, Lugh realized Abby had been short and cranky since Wyn's father and coven had shown up. He grabbed her arm and led her into the back room. "Okay, you're mad."

She sighed and made a rune in the air.

A quick tingle of magic washed over Lugh. "What was that?"

"A circle of silence." She shook her head. "It'll be nice when you know more magic."

"What?" Lugh listened hard and the sounds from the front of the store were still there. "I can still hear them."

"But they can't hear you." Bran looked up from the cat bed on the shelf. The cat didn't move from the shelf.

"If they can't hear us, how can Bran?" Lugh asked before Abby could answer.

She pursed her lips, like she was trying to not snap at him. "He's your familiar. Magic won't block him being able to hear you."

"Okay. So tell me why you're mad today." It made sense that Bran could hear him, so he turned his focus back to Abby.

She glanced at the beaded curtain. "We shouldn't need the Wiccans here to protect us. We're more powerful than they are."

"So. And you might be, but I'm still learning here." Lugh didn't want to admit that after the Shadow Magi, he was thankful for anyone who wanted to help keep him safe.

"Yeah." She let out a long sigh. "I guess there is that."

"Plus, Bryan probably thinks he's keeping Wyn safe. That should count for something. I think it's great he wants to be part of Wyn's life and that he cares what happens." Lugh frowned for a second. "I miss having my dad around and caring what happens to me."

Abby shrugged. "My dad was never around. I don't even know who he is."

Although Lugh had wanted to ask, he'd never done so. He knew a lot of kids in school that only had one parent, and like himself, some of them didn't like to talk about it. The situation was just too painful. He'd always figured that Abby or Catherine would tell him and his mom someday when it was a good time for them. "What happened?"

"Beltane." Abby made it sound like it was something Lugh should understand.

He did remember the term, it was a spring pagan holiday. But he didn't know enough to understand why that should be a good reason for Abby to not know who her father was. "And…" he prompted.

"It's a bit like Vegas, what happens at Beltane stays at Beltane." She sighed again. "It's a fertility holiday. It's also the time when magical babies are conceived. It makes sense that I'd be conceived at a Beltane ritual. Actually, at lot of Magi are conceived during holidays. I bet you were conceived at Samhain or Yule, depending on if you were early or not."

Lugh didn't really want to talk about himself. "No clue. So you're just in a snit because the Wiccans have showed up to lend a hand and be protective?"

She gave an overly dramatic sigh. "Yeah. I guess so. I mean, look, I'm supposed to be keeping watch on the area while Mom's gone. This makes it look like I can't do my job."

It was another concept Lugh wasn't used to hearing. "Keep watch on the area?"

"Yeah. Mom monitors the other magic users in the area. She's tied into the paths."

That didn't make a lot of sense, or there was something Lugh was missing. "Then how didn't she know about the Shadow Magi?"

"She has been trying to figure that out too. All she's been able to come up with is they had some kind of talisman or something that allowed them to move about undetected. But normally if a Magus accesses the paths or even does magic in about a hundred miles of here, she knows about it. While she's gone, I'm supposed to be her proxy, but so far, I haven't picked up on much until that woman scanned us. I wasn't really worried about it, since magic isn't so common and there's not a ton of people using it. Mom can recognize everyone in town by their magical signature."

Yeah, it was all news to Lugh. "Wow. That must be a lot to take in. Will we all be able to do that when we get older?"

Abby nodded. "Most likely. The Magi all control different territories. The ones who show up for holidays with us are all in adjacent territories to ours."

"I've still got a lot to learn about my life, don't I?" Lugh did his best to not sound overwhelmed at the idea. It was a bit more than what Catherine had told him up to that point.

"Hey, Abby." Wyn stuck his head through the beads. "Need you to run a credit card. His strip isn't working and I can't figure out how to manually enter it."

Abby reversed the rune she'd drawn earlier. "Coming."

Wyn looked between the two of them.

As Lugh walked past him, following in Abby's wake, he leaned close. "Trying to get her less pissy."

"Oh." Wyn nodded and went with them.

The rest of the day, Abby seemed in a slightly better mood, until her mother called to say she was going to stay in Colorado Springs overnight and Abby needed to spend the night at Lugh's house.

12

Sleepover

"Abby, I think you'll be fine on the couch," Lugh's mom said as she carried an armload of blankets to the living room.

"Should be." Abby replied.

Lugh watched his cousin who'd been quiet since their talk that afternoon. It wasn't like her to get silent. Well, not silent exactly, but she'd had a lot less to say than normal, and when Aunt Catherine had called the shop after calling Lugh's mother to make sure it was okay for her to crash with them that night, she'd gotten downright hostile to everyone but Lugh and his mom.

After his mom had the couch made up into a bed for Abby, she headed for her bathroom. "Okay, you two don't stay up all night. You've got school in the morning and neither of you are to miss any classes."

"Yes, Mom," Lugh replied.

"Yes, Aunt Margret," Abby echoed.

Once her door was closed, Lugh looked at Abby. "Okay, what did your mom say that's got you madder than you were at the shop?"

Abby shook her head and settled on the couch, punching the pillow a couple of times. "Not madder. Worried." Morrigan hopped up next to her and started kneading the blanket for a moment before circling around and lying down tight against Abby. "Mom said she can't find any trace of Espe's family. Since she grew up in Colorado Springs, she knew them. They don't live where they used to. She's trying to find a couple of the other Magi in the area, but so far, no luck. She was the last member of our family to leave the area. She's worried something might've happened to them."

Lugh plopped down in the arm chair next to the couch. "What would've happened to them?"

"With what we've had to deal with around here, maybe dark magic." Abby shrugged. "I don't know."

"Give me a minute." Lugh got up and went to get his laptop. He barely glanced at Bran curled up asleep on his pillow on Lugh's bed as he flipped on the light long enough to find his laptop and head back to the living room.

"What's that for?" Abby asked, then stifled a yawn.

"Just because Catherine can't find them using magic, doesn't mean we can't help her out from here with technology." He turned on the laptop and waited for it to boot up. "Maybe it's because I'm late getting into the magical life, but sometimes I wonder why we don't use technology more."

"Because it's not as effective as magic." Abby stroked Morrigan.

"Says who?" Lugh wished his laptop booted faster. It would make his life a lot speedier.

Abby shrugged. "Lots of people."

"Well, in this case it might be better." As the splash screen cleared so he could see his desktop, Lugh pulled up his browser. "Okay, what was Espe's last name again? I remember it started with a C."

Abby yawned again. "Coleman."

"Do we know her folks' names?" Lugh entered *Espe Coleman* into the search engine.

"Nope, never heard of her until today. Mom might know."

"Give me a second." Lugh was surprised when he started getting hits. According to the news articles he was finding, Espe Coleman had gone missing with her cocker spaniel in Colorado Springs about twenty-five years ago. There was a picture. His breath caught. It was the glowing girl from camp. "Okay. So, there is a record of her going missing twenty-five years ago." He read through several articles. "Says her parents are Clara and Peter Coleman."

He entered their names into the search engine. "Okay, looks like Peter died in a car accident a couple of years ago, and Clara was killed when her house exploded." He read that article very closely. "They say it was a gas leak."

Abby leaned over his shoulder and shook her head. "Shadow Magi. It has to be."

"Both or just the house explosion?" Lugh straightened so he was hunched over his laptop.

"Definitely the house explosion." Abby stood and paced around the room. "Maybe the car accident too. It's easy to make things look like accidents."

"Okay, but I thought you said Catherine said there were different people living in the Coleman's house. If that's the truth, then it couldn't have exploded." Lugh was trying to apply logic to the situation. He'd figured out a couple of months earlier, that often when the going got strange, logic was the best thing he had to try and explain things, even if he had to move magic into the world of logic, which its existence often seemed to defy, even if the actual working of magic were fairly logical.

"Can you check addresses? Maybe they moved." Abby didn't stop pacing. "If Mom's in danger, we should try and get some of this information to her. It might be useful."

Lugh quickly complied with her request. "Having the proper information is always a good idea." When he managed to find the address the Colemans had been living at when Espe disappeared and compared that to where Clara had been killed, they didn't match.

Abby pulled out her phone and speed dialed. "Hey Mom….Yeah, I'm over at Lugh's…look we're doing a bit of research online. Trying to help…I don't think a computer search is going to show up on anybody's radar…It was Lugh's idea…but anyway, it looks like the Colemans moved after Espe disappeared. But they're both dead. Mr. Coleman died in a car accident and Mrs. Coleman died when her house had a gas leak and exploded…yeah, that's what I thought, too."

Lugh could guess at what his aunt was telling Abby, but he wished Bran was in the living room with them instead of napping in the bedroom. He and the cat could link up and listen in. With a situation as dire as Magi dying, he didn't exactly think it would be deemed as eavesdropping.

"Okay, hold on." Abby stopped and stared at Lugh. "She wants you to check on a couple other names. Magi she knows were in the Springs within the past few years."

Happy to do more to help the cause, Lugh nodded. "Okay. Give 'em to me."

After she gave him each name, he put it into the search engine. There were three names. None of them still lived in Colorado Springs. Two had died on the same night, but on different sides of town during a blizzard the previous winter. The other one had moved to Kansas City five years earlier.

"You're sure?" Abby asked after she relayed Lugh's information. "Wow, that's scary….so you'll be home before we get out of school tomorrow?...Okay, see you then." She disconnected the call and plopped back on the couch, seeming much more cheerful than she'd been most of the day. "I love being helpful."

"Me too," Lugh agreed. "So she'll be home tomorrow."

Abby nodded. "She's going to check a couple of the Magi in Denver on her way back. She figures they're okay since Tom hasn't said anything about any of them being missing. He's the Magus closest to Denver who we see on a regular basis."

"Right." Lugh remembered Tom; he'd been there the night the Shadow Magi attacked the circle. It had been Lugh's first circle, when he received his focus ring. Tom's familiar was a ferret; then Bran had smelled a ferret in the house where the Shadow Magi had taken Abby and Wyn after they were kidnapped. He didn't have anything to go on but his gut, but he didn't trust the guy, even if he was part of a circle of Light Magi.

"Now what?" Abby asked, then yawned.

"I think we should probably hit the bed. Like Mom said, we've got school tomorrow." Lugh stifled his own yawn. Working in the store had been a lot more tiring than he wanted to let on. He wouldn't have thought moving around helping customers all day would've hit him like it had, but he was ready to join Bran on the bed and get to sleep.

"You haven't done many sleepovers have you?" She grinned.

He shook his head. "I think sleepovers are more a girl thing than a boy thing. I mean I did campout in a friend's backyard a couple of times back in Florida. It wasn't like camping with Wyn was. We could run into the house anytime we needed anything."

"Okay, so boys campout and girls sleepover. What did you do on your campouts?" She settled back on the couch and started paying attention to Morrigan again.

"Told ghost stories. Had smores over a camp fire. Talked about girls."

"Then I'm guessing the boys back in Florida didn't know you're gay."

Lugh shrugged. "I was still figuring things out. I came out before I moved here. Even dated one of the guys on the football team."

"And now you've got Wyn." Abby stopped petting Morrigan and leaned a little toward Lugh, like she was a conspirator or something. "You know he's quite the catch around town, don't you?"

"And I'm happy I caught him." Lugh didn't think there was anything about his relationship with Wyn Abby didn't know. "So what about you? Haven't seen you watching any of the boys around school."

Abby frowned a little bit and settled back against the couch cushions and resumed petting Morrigan. "Some of them are pretty, but none of them are Magi. Other than Wyn, none of them even follow the old ways." She shook her head. "Nothing for me to really do with any of them rather than just look."

"You know, you could get a feel for dating." Lugh closed his laptop and set it on the coffee table. "Might at least get you ready for meeting the right Magus." He'd known Abby was a bit prejudiced about Magi dating regular humans. It might have been because his own parents were a mixed couple, but Lugh didn't see the problem with it, other than his mother's fear of magic and the way that seemed to complicate his life.

"Nope. If they aren't magical, I'm waiting. Mom's talking about all of us going to a gathering this summer. Maybe I'll meet a nice Magus boy there. We'll see."

"All of us? What kind of gathering?" Lugh hadn't heard anything about a family trip in the summer, but then he wasn't as privileged to what Catherine was thinking as Abby.

"Well." Abby straightened and took on her common air of authority. "Every few years most of the Magi in the country get together for a big ritual. It's normally over Litha."

It was another of the words he didn't know. "Litha?"

She frowned. "You really need to be reading more of the books at the shop. There's more to magic than just making the right rune and keeping in tune with your ring and Bran. Litha is what we call Midsummer. It's the longest day of the year. I think we do the gathering then as opposed to at Yule because more of us kids are out of school in the summer. Although with year-round school catching on, that might be changing. Or it could be so people can be more comfortable outside. Since we camp there, it's not as cold as it would be in the winter."

"And I can see some of the familiars preferring that." Lugh could just hear Bran complain the whole time if they tried to go camping in the middle of winter.

Abby laughed. "Morrigan agrees with you. She doesn't want to go camping in the winter."

"Right." As Lugh thought about it. He realized he hoped he could go. It would be nice to meet even more Magi than he had already. Then a thought struck him. "But this gathering is only for Light Magi, not Shadow Magi, right?"

"Right. I don't think any Shadow Magi would have the balls to show up at the gathering. It would be downright suicidal."

Before Lugh could ask Abby anything more about the gathering, Bran came barreling into the living room, moving like a streaming gray comet. *"Lugh, she's here!"*

He stopped and stared at the cat. "Who's here?"

"The Goth woman from the shop," Abby hissed. "Morrigan feels her too."

13

Unexpected Attack

Lugh grabbed Bran. "Do you know where she is?"

"Coming down the sidewalk toward the house." Bran's tail stood out like a bottle brush.

"We've got to protect Mom," Lugh looked down the hall, toward the bathroom. The light was still on under the door. He figured his mother was still taking her nightly bath.

"I'll put up a shield," Abby said. She rushed to the bathroom, her ring began to glow and Lugh didn't bother watching as she cast the protections to keep his mother safe.

He went to the window beside the door. Taking a second to turn off the living room lights, Lugh prepared for the possibility the Goth woman might be coming to cause trouble. But he'd never been followed home before. His heart pounded as Bran growled in his arms.

The flow of magic died back, indicating Abby had finished her shield. Out on the sidewalk, the woman cocked her head, like she'd also felt Abby casting the spell. The action sent a shiver down Lugh's spine.

"Can Shadow Magi sense our magic?" Lugh muttered.

"Once you're attuned to magic, you can feel it being used," Bran replied. "Regardless of the kind of magic it is."

"What's she doing?" Abby whispered from right behind Lugh, causing him to jump slightly.

"I think she felt you casting the shield." Lugh kept his voice low, hoping it wouldn't carry out the house and down the walk. He did his best to not move his hand and jiggle the curtain. Try as he might, he couldn't see any sign of her having a familiar. But as he learned with the Shadow Magi, not all familiars were as large as cats, dogs and hawks. There were a lot of smaller familiars that could easily hide in a pocket, and stay undetected, even by people who knew what to look for.

"Then she knows magic," Abby replied, still keeping her voice low. "I can't feel anything happening." She paused, then continued. "Neither can Morrigan."

"I can't feel her doing anything right this moment," Bran confirmed.

"So, what do we do?" Lugh felt weird with the lights out staring at the woman standing on the sidewalk. It felt cowardly. He should've been out there confronting the woman. He'd been successful in defeating the Shadow Magi months earlier. But he knew that had been dumb luck. There was still so much he had to learn.

"We wait," Abby whispered. "Maybe she was just walking down the street and felt your residual magic."

"Do you really believe that?" Lugh might've believed in coincidence a few months ago, but not anymore. Magic didn't work that way.

Abby shook her head.

After a minute, the woman moved her hand and walked toward the house.

Bran's growl rose in volume. *"She's doing something!"*

Lugh didn't really need him to say anything. He could feel the magic coming his way. It was softer and subtler than when Abby cast her shield.

"What kind of magic is she doing?" Lugh hoped Abby had some idea.

"No clue. Use the shielding techniques Mom's been teaching you." Even as she spoke, Lugh felt the tingle from magic of a shield spring up around Abby.

With a deep breath, he tried to still his mind and focus on his ring to bring up his own shield. But he couldn't believe someone would be so brazen as to attack him in his own home. It wasn't right. His thoughts raced and he struggled to connect with the easy rhythm of the smoky quartz in his ring.

"Lugh. Relax. It's not going to work if you don't relax." Abby's voice had the gentle tone of Catherine.

He forced out another breath.

"I'm right here," Bran's presence filled his mind as the cat's growl turned to a purr. *"Let me help you relax so you can make your shield. Her magic is soft but strong. We can do this."*

With Bran bolstering him, Lugh reached deep inside himself, connected with the pulse of his ring and formed the protective barrier he needed to. He managed to get it shaped the way he needed as something strong stuck it.

Lugh stumbled backward from the impact. "What was that?"

"Magical bolt." Abby did something so fast he couldn't follow her motions. Magic roared out of her. "She's definitely not friendly."

Not seeing the need to hide in the house anymore, Lugh flung the door open and stepped out onto the stoop. He felt stronger just by stepping out of the shadows and trying to be more active.

"Who are you?" Lugh shouted at the woman. "What do you want from us?"

The woman frowned and staggered a couple of steps as Abby sent another volley of magic her direction. She straightened, squared her shoulders and advanced on Lugh. "The time of light grows dim. Shadows lengthen and you don't even realize it." Her hands moved in a blur and magic flowed out, but Lugh couldn't catch a flash from a ring like he'd grown used to seeing when Catherine or Abby did their spells. There was something different in the way she worked.

He jerked as the magical bolt passed by his shield and hit the house, knocking a circle of paint off where it hit.

"What?" Lugh had never seen magic affect the physical world like that before. He'd seen it affect the magic users and thus impact the world by making them fall, stumble or worse.

"She's not a Magus!" Bran shrieked.

The woman continued toward them, her hands moving again.

"Not a Magus?" Lugh fought to settle his mind enough to expand his shield. He didn't want her taking holes out of his house.

"Hit her the same time I do!" Abby shouted as she walked up next to him.

"With what?" Lugh hadn't learned any offensive magics.

"I'll show you." Bran still sounded frantic. In Lugh's mind, he saw the runes he needed to draw in the air to make the magical bolts Abby made.

It looked simple. "Okay. Let's do this."

Another bolt from the woman bounced off Lugh's expanded shield. He felt the blow. His head throbbed and he knew he'd have a headache when their battle was over. He often got headaches from magic use. Catherine always said it was part of the price they pay for their power. Lugh considered it a small price considering the difference it made in his life.

He drew the rune and pushed power out through it. The energy flared through his link with Bran. A huge ram of energy shot out from him; it was just seconds before Abby unleashed another volley. Together, they forced the woman to retreat two steps.

"No!" Espe and her cocker spaniel appeared on the walk between Lugh, Abby and the strange woman. Ghostly blue lighting arrowed out from her hands as the dog barked frantically. "You will *not* hurt Colin!" Her volley hit lanced through the woman's protections and made her fly backward.

She was back on her feet with frightening grace. Frowning, her hands blurred. "You're strong, but young and won't always be defended." She disappeared.

"Espe, thanks for the save." Lugh started toward her, but she and her familiar vanished as their blue glow faded into nothing.

Lugh looked at Abby. His cousin was pale and wobbling. His own head pounded like crazy. "What was she?"

"I don't…" Abby's eyes rolled back in her head and she collapsed.

Abby Down

14

Lugh somehow managed to catch Abby before she hit the sidewalk. She was like a wet pool noodle in his grasp. He lowered her down to the ground and knelt next to her. He touched her throat and felt a pulse. That was a good sign.

"Bran, go get Mom!" Lugh hoped his mother was out of the bath and Bran could get to her.

The gray cat streaked up the stairs as Morrigan pushed against Abby and mewed pitifully.

"Mom will be here in a minute and everything'll be alright," Lugh said, more for himself than Morrigan. He had no idea what had happened. If the strange woman had attacked Abby, he should've felt something. But he'd been busy helping Abby assault the woman while trying to defend them. There was so much about magic he still didn't understand. He must've missed something.

"We're coming!" Bran shouted as he bounded off the step and landed next to Lugh.

"Lugh, are you out here?" His mother called from the house.

"Mom! Abby's hurt!" He glanced behind him. She stood in the doorway, her robe billowing behind her in the night breeze.

His mother was in instant action. "What happened?" She was at his side almost as fast as Bran had been.

"The woman from the shop today showed up." Lugh hated admitting there had been danger, but there was no way he could put any kind of positive spin on Abby lying unconscious on the sidewalk. "We defended the house. She attacked. We chased her off, then Abby collapsed."

"Not good." His mother felt Abby's neck. "She's still alive. We need to get her into the house." She stood and then pulled Abby into a fireman's carry over her shoulder. "Come on, cats too. Everyone in the house."

The fact that his mother wasn't yelling at him about them being attacked at home, gave Lugh a bit of hope things might end up okay. He ran ahead of her and held the door open so she could get through without a problem. Bran and Morrigan dashed ahead of them and were on the back of the couch by the time they entered the living room.

"Lugh, call your aunt before we decide if I need to take her to the ER. Maybe Catherine'll know something *you* can do to wake her." His mom lowered Abby to the couch, and Morrigan instantly jumped down next to her and curled up next to her head, purring so loudly it was audible several feet away.

Lugh yanked his cell phone out of his jeans pocket and speed dialed Catherine. He was almost surprised when she picked up on the second ring.

"Lugh, what's wrong? You should be in bed." She sounded sleepy.

Trying to not leave anything out, Lugh explained everything that had happened. It came out quickly and he just hoped Catherine understood what he was saying.

When he paused, she said. "Lugh, put your mother on for me."

He glanced at the couch. His mom was looking in Abby's eyes with a small flashlight. "Mom, Catherine would like to talk to you." He held out the phone.

"Okay." She set the flashlight on the table and took the phone. "Yes, Catherine…At the moment, she's unresponsive, but her pupils are dilating correctly, her breathing and heart rate seem normal…are you sure?...of course…I thought there might be something Lugh and the cats could try to wake her…oh…I hadn't thought of that…okay. I'll hand you back to Lugh." She offered Lugh the phone. "There's something she wants you to try."

Lugh took the phone back. A knot formed in his stomach. He'd been hoping it was just going to be medical and not magical. He didn't like the idea of holding Abby's life in his hand and if he had to use magic to wake her up, that was exactly what he was going to be doing. "Yes, Catherine."

His aunt sighed. "Okay. It sounds to me like Abby magically overextended herself. It's nothing a bit of sleep and food won't cure, but we need to be sure. What I want you to do is get Bran and Morrigan to help you scan Abby. We've worked on some of this already. You know what her aura feels like. You need to make sure it's intact, then you need to find her magical center and make sure it's okay. If she has overexerted herself, it might be hard to find since it's going to be basically depleted. Both Bran and Morrigan will be able to help you do this. It's basic familiar magic. Give the phone back to your mother and tell her what you find and she'll relay it to me."

"Okay." Wishing he had a more expensive phone that had speaker phone on it, he gave his mom back the phone and took a deep breath, centering himself the way he'd been taught. It only took him a couple of steps to be at the edge of the couch. Sitting on the coffee table, he let himself fall into synch with his focus ring and Bran before he touched Abby.

Her hand was colder than he remembered it being. Then he tried to remember the last time he'd held her hand. They were cousins, it wasn't something he did very often. But they'd been practicing lending each other power for magic.

"Morrigan's here with us," Bran said, reminding Lugh to focus on the task they were supposed to be doing.

"She's far away," said a sultry female voice who had to be Morrigan. *"I hope we can reach her."*

Lugh started with looking at Abby's aura. Hers had been one of the first he'd ever seen. He studied it. The pale blue glow with sparks of gold and silver was much tighter against her skin than it should've been. But it appeared to be complete. "Aura is tight, but looks like it's all there," he said so his mother could tell Catherine.

With a deep breath, Lugh pushed his thoughts into Abby. He had no idea how to find the center of her magic. He knew were his was, it was in his chest, just below his heart.

"Let us help." Bran was a sleek comforting presence in his mind.

On the other side of his thoughts, Morrigan felt much larger and more dangerous. "This way." She took the lead, pulling them deeper into Abby.

It was a very strange sensation. Lugh was aware of his own body, but seemed to be filling Abby's too. Her heart rate was a steady pulse in his mind as was her breathing. Other energies running through her seemed a lot lighter than the similar channels Lugh was just starting to get used to feeling in his own body. It was down one of these lightly pulsing channels, Morrigan led them. If Lugh hadn't already learned how to follow his own magical energies, he'd have never been able to sense what Morrigan was leading him toward.

The core of Abby's power throbbed weakly, like a flashing headlamp whose battery was dying. A jolt of fear shot through Lugh, and he had to push it back as he began to focus on his own body. He didn't want to think about Abby dying. He'd just found her and Catherine. He'd recently lost his father. He couldn't lose any more family.

"She's very weak," Morrigan said. The cat reached out and touched Abby's core. The throbbing power instantly strengthened.

"Should we try to give her power?" Lugh asked.

In the distance he heard his mother repeat the question into the phone, although he'd been asking Bran.

"I don't see what it will hurt," Bran replied. *"She's very weak. She's draining a lot from Morrigan. But that's one of the things we familiars are here for, strengthening our Magus."*

"Be careful doing that," Lugh's mother said. "She might pull too much out of you if she's too weak."

Lugh didn't care. He had to do what he could to help Abby. As Bran started purring, he pushed his magic out, visualizing it like water flowing from him to Abby's magical core. It hit Abby's core and the throbbing strengthened again. The dim light of the core brightened and became steadier. He kept up his efforts until he felt lightheaded. His hold on Abby slipped.

"Lugh!" Bran shouted. *"Let go! You're giving her too much!"* Bran was doing something to break their connection.

"Stop!" Morrigan screeched.

Something hit Lugh in the chest, throwing him back against the coffee table. His head throbbed and he looked up into Morrigan's face. The cat didn't say anything, she just leapt back to the couch and curled up next to Abby again.

"What happened?" Abby murmured.

Lugh straightened.

"That's what I was about to ask." His mother offered him a hand to sit up again. "Why did Morrigan attack Lugh?"

"Well," —Lugh rubbed his pained head which he figured was hurting more from magic than Morrigan breaking his probe of Abby— "I think she was stopping me from giving Abby too much magic." He yawned, suddenly very tired.

"That's right," Bran said. His voice in Lugh's head drove another spike of pain through him.

Lugh stroked his cat. "Please don't talk to me right now. My head hurts too much."

Abby sighed. "Okay. Morrigan just updated me." She looked at Lugh's mom. "Aunt Margaret, can I talk to Mom for a second? Then I want to sleep."

Frowning slightly, his mother handed her the phone.

"I'll be fine, Mom…No, I don't know what she was, only that she isn't a Magus. Her magic is all wrong, and I'm pretty sure she didn't have a familiar."

"I didn't sense or smell one either," Bran said. The words sent fresh pain through Lugh's head.

"Bran." He rubbed his temple and glared at the cat.

Bran purred and pushed against Lugh's hand, as if that would be enough apology for making his headache worse.

"Whatever she is, she's powerful," Abby continued. "Yeah, I agree with Lugh, I think we drove her off. If we're lucky…Mom, do we really…okay I'll leave that up to Margaret and Bryan…yes, I really should get to sleep." She yawned. "And I promise to have a good breakfast in the morning…really? You're sure? Okay, sounds good…Did you tell Aunt Margaret?" She held the phone out to Lugh's mother. "She's got one last thing."

Lugh's mom took the phone. "Yes…Do you really think that's necessary? Okay, you know more about this sort of thing than I do…Yes, I'll call Bryan and we'll work something out…Alright, we'll see you tomorrow." She ended the call and looked at Lugh and Abby. "Looks like you two get a skip day tomorrow." Her eyes hardened as she focused more on Lugh. "Don't think this is going to become a habit, young man."

As tired as he was, Lugh figured most of the day was going to be spent sleeping. There wasn't a lot of fun in that, and he'd end up with extra homework on Wednesday. He yawned again. "I won't."

15

History Isn't Always Pretty

Lugh sat on his porch and watched Aunt Catherine walk back and forth across the spot on the sidewalk where they'd faced the strange woman. He used his magical sight so he could catch everything she was doing. Although it wasn't defensive magic, the spells she was using were things he hadn't seen before, and after the attack he was more determined than ever to learn everything he could, as fast as he could. He didn't want to be caught without important knowledge.

"She's very good at this kind of thing," Bran said. *"Bast says she's one of the best in the country, but Bast is probably biased."*

Lugh nodded in agreement. "I think most familiars are biased where their Magi are concerned."

"Maybe." Bran shifted a little bit on the porch, the spot of sunshine he'd been lying in had moved slightly and he followed it.

The door behind them opened, and Abby walked out. Her red hair was wet, like she'd just gotten out of the shower. Morrigan paced at her side. "She find anything yet?" She sat next to Lugh on the step.

"Not that she's told me." Lugh turned his attention back to his aunt. "I guess we should be lucky it's in the middle of the week and most everyone is at work. It bet if this was a weekend, we'd have people stopping to ask what she was doing."

Abby shrugged. "Maybe, maybe not. Hard to tell a lot of the time. Remember how most non-magical folks just let their brain see what it wants to see. They'd probably decide she was looking for a lost earring or something while talking on a blue-tooth headset."

Catherine sighed and turned toward them. "And you two sitting there talking isn't helping me figure out what happened here last night, or who, or what your attacker was."

"Sorry," they said in eerie unison and Lugh immediately hoped they'd never do it again. Although he liked his cousin, he didn't like the idea of being so in synch with her that they could say the same thing at the same time. It was too strange.

"I can't get anything concrete." Catherine leaned against the porch rail next to the step. "I can tell there was a magical battle. I find four signatures. The two of you are obvious. The other two…they are both things I've never encountered before." She sighed. "I'm going to guess that the one with the least impact on the area, and that feels vaguely like a Magus, is Espe. The other…it's raw power is frightening. I am very proud of you both for defending against it. You say it appeared human?"

"Right." Lugh nodded. "There wasn't anything that suggested she wasn't human."

"But her magic wasn't Magi magic and was a lot more powerful than any Wiccan I've ever encountered," Abby added.

Catherine shook her head. "Definitely not Wiccan. Plus if it had been, I think Bryan would've said something since he was here until I arrived. We're lucky the magical community around here works well together."

"We're also fairly small," Abby said.

"Yeah. Wyn's disappointed he had to go to school today and we didn't," Lugh threw in. He'd been getting texts from Wyn every hour as he moved from class to class. He wished Wyn could be there with them, but Bryan had been adamant that Wyn not miss any school. Since he hadn't been involved in the magical battle, he didn't get time off to recover, even if he had been on the phone with Lugh for more than an hour after the event.

"Gwydyon will get over it," Catherine said. "And the two of you will be in school tomorrow. Abby's looking much better after sleeping into the afternoon." She paced a little bit. "I'm going to need to do something really nice for Bryan's coven after this is all over. They didn't have to come down and make sure everything went smoothly yesterday after that woman left the shop. Her appearance, combined with my not finding anything in Colorado Springs yesterday has me worried."

"So you weren't able to find any of the other Magi?" Abby stroked Morrigan after the cat hopped into her lap.

"None. When we lived there, I knew of seven different Magi spread over the city. True, three of those were in the military and probably didn't stay around long. But I sent out magical probes and it's like the area is devoid of magic users. The raw natural power is still there, but there's nobody tapping into it." She shook her head and stared at the ground. "We should've been made aware of a void like that."

"What about Denver?" Abby asked.

"I've got calls out to see what, if anything is going on there, but so far, I haven't been able to talk to anyone, just leave messages. If you hadn't been attacked, I was going to stop and see what's going on, make sure folks are alright. But the state of Colorado Springs makes me think someone is attacking light workers."

"We know the Shadow Magi are," Lugh said. He wanted to get up and pace with his aunt, but didn't want to add to the nervous energy around them. It was all he could do to sit still.

"Yes, but I was hoping we might've been an early attack in their plan," Catherine said. "I would've like to have gotten some information out of them, but that didn't happen."

"Do things like this happen all the time?" Lugh's mother came out of the house.

"Like the attack last night, or the Shadow Magi?" Catherine asked.

"Yes." Lugh's mother caught the screen door and closed it quietly. "Both. It's almost like you're at constant war."

"Yes and no." Catherine stopped pacing at the bottom step. "Let's go inside."

"*Can I stay out here?*" Bran asked. "*The sunlight is nice and warm. We might not have many warm days after today.*"

"I suppose we can," Lugh's mom said, replying to Catherine's suggestion.

Lugh looked at Catherine. "Do you think it's safe to leave Bran out? He wants to stay in the sunlight."

Catherine chuckled. It was the first happy sound she'd made since she came back from her failed trip. "Sure. The sunlight would do us all some good, but to answer your mother's question fully it's going to take a little while and I'd rather not risk being overheard."

Morrigan and Bast joined Bran in the sunbeam on the porch while the humans went into the house.

"It's a fairly simple question," Lugh's mom said once they were in the living room.

Catherine gestured for them to all take seats. "But it's not a very simple answer. Magi have a long and complicated history. We're directly tied to the balance of light and dark on Earth. There have always been light workers and there have always been shadow workers. But from time to time the shadows try and gain an upper hand, throwing things out of balance. The Earth herself responds when the imbalance becomes too great."

"What do you mean by that?" Lugh's mother asked, her face set in a hard mask that told Lugh she wasn't at all happy with what she was hearing.

"Drought, famine, plague, floods, global warming and cooling, these are all natural phenomena, but they can often be traced back to the natural balance of things being thrown out of whack."

"Wait a minute," Lugh interrupted. "Are you saying that the icecaps are melting because there aren't enough light workers in the world?"

Catherine shrugged. "Maybe. I figured it was due to greenhouse gasses."

"Then how do we tell the difference between things like greenhouse gasses and Shadow Magi?" Lugh was getting incredibly confused.

"Actually it's very hard to tell now. Back in time, before we really understood science, black magic was blamed for a lot of different things, often stuff that magic never touched." Catherine sighed and fiddled with the cuff of her light-weight jacket. "That's why it gets really complicated trying to tell magic from science and sometimes, vice versa. And truth be told, I don't know if anyone can identify something that was the tipping point between an event being related to an imbalance in the magics and the natural phenomena being out of kilter. The thing we do know is that if there aren't enough Magi in the world, dark things happen."

"Have there ever been too many light workers?" Lugh's mother asked before he could.

Catherine shook her head. "Not that I've ever heard of. But I suppose it's possible for the scales to swing the other way, but we only hear about things when they go bad for us. If things are going good for us, we don't hear about them."

"And when things are balanced, I take it you're not needed as much?" Lugh's mom asked.

"Right. That's when we manage to live peaceful lives. Unfortunately, I don't think this is one of those peaceful times."

An idea hit Lugh and he blurted it out before he gave it much time to process. "Do you think the Shadow Magi had anything to do with Dad's death? Isn't it possible he didn't just have a boating accident, but someone wrecked his boat?"

"It is possible," Catherine agreed. "We'll never know for sure. First it happened at sea. All traces of the magical residue are gone. Salt water makes holding magic together almost impossible, unless you're one of the ones who's really attuned to it. But a Magus would've had to be on the scene quickly to look it over and make sure. Even without salt water, magic fades over time."

"Which is why you were looking for clues on the sidewalk as soon as you made sure Abby was safely sleeping," Lugh said. He would've liked a more definitive answer to his question, but figured it was the best he was going to get. The more he learned about magic, the more he kept hoping he could find a way to save his dad, or at the very least avenge him if someone had caused the boating accident.

Catherine nodded. "Exactly. Like a policeman looking at the scene of a crime, we get more information the sooner we get to the scene."

Lugh's phone beeped with an incoming message. Normally he'd let it go, but his gut tightened as the beep sounded and he'd been expecting a text from Wyn, it was about time for him to be going to his last class.

Someone's doing magic. Strong magic. Come quick!

"We've got to go." Lugh showed the phone to Catherine.

"This isn't good." She looked at Abby. "You stay here with Margaret. You're still recovering from last night. Lugh and I have to see what's happening at the high school!"

16

Sprung Trap

"You cats should wait out here," Catherine said as she pulled into the school parking lot. "But stay hidden and on guard. If we've got someone casting spells in school, they could be searching for Lugh and Abby, and that means familiars as well."

"I should be at your side," Bran objected. *"But I'll listen to Catherine."* He slipped out of Lugh's lap and under the seat. He barely fit. He wasn't the small kitten he'd been when Lugh first found him.

"You'll be the first to know if there's trouble." Lugh reached down and scratched his head. He'd feel a lot better with Bran at his side, but understood Catherine's logic. Plus with school about to let out, they'd attract a lot less attention if they didn't have the cats with them. He wasn't sure if he was going to get into trouble for being there when he'd called in sick or not.

Bast slipped down into the floor board and curled up, looking at the window Catherine was leaving cracked.

"If you two need to run, the window's open, plus that way you won't get too hot." Catherine opened the door and got out.

Lugh followed her lead. The feathery touch of magic caught him off guard and he stared at Catherine. She was finishing up a rune and the magic was cascading over him. "What did you do?"

"A major shield. It makes you invisible to human eyes, electronics, and magic. You're supposed to be home sick. I'd rather not have any major questions about you being here." She continued walking toward the front doors. "I can already feel some magic coming from inside. Abby's right, this isn't Magus magic, or Wiccan. I've felt it before, but can't remember where or when."

The final bell for school rang as they entered the door, and Lugh braced himself for the flood of humanity that was about to wash over them. Being invisible was going to make not getting stepped on harder than normal.

Catherine hurried through the door to the office before it shut behind a teacher. It was one Lugh had seen around school, but didn't know her name. As the door closed, the thunder of feet hurrying out of school rumbled down the hall. Lugh had never been so thankful to be in the office.

In the relative calm, Catherine sat in one of the chairs next to the door, and Lugh thought it was odd no one was asking her why she was there. She closed her eyes and the tingle of seeking magic made Lugh's eyes hurt. It was a spell he had learned recently and it always made his eyes hurt.

In an effort to ignore the sensation, he pulled out his phone and texted Wyn.

We're in the office. Catherine is doing a seeking spell. Got any input?

Wyn's reply was almost instant.

The gym I think. I'm heading your way.

Lugh grinned as he typed.

Won't be able to see me. Catherine made me invisible.

A wide mouth emoji started Wyn's reply.

Is she invisible?

Even though Lugh could still see her, they still hadn't been bothered by any of the staff, even though the main secretary was sitting at her desk across from the counter and kept looking their way. It was way too weird.

I can see her, but no one is reacting to her being here in the office. It's like they don't see her.

Cool.

Wyn walked through the door, looked at Catherine. Before he could say or do anything, the secretary who'd been ignoring Catherine stood and stepped over to the counter.

"Mr. Chambers, is there anything I can help you with?"

For a second, Wyn looked confused, then he walked up to the counter. "I was hoping to get Lugh McNeal's homework. I told him I'd stop by the office and pick it up for the class he and I don't have together."

She sighed. "Normally it has to be a parent."

"I think Lugh's mom is home today if you need to ask her. I can wait." Wyn leaned against the counter.

"Give me a moment." She hurried back to her computer and after a second picked up her phone.

Before she turned back, Catherine's spell ended. "Come on Lugh," she whispered and stood.

There was a teacher coming through the door and Catherine waited, then slipped out. They hurried down the hall toward the gym.

"Shouldn't we wait for Wyn?" Lugh did his best to keep up with her, but she was walking fast, as if rushing to a fire.

"No. He's not prepared to deal with this kind of magic. He'll be safer getting your homework." Catherine didn't break stride as they rounded the corner and all but ran past the cafeteria. Luckily they were deep enough into the school that the flow of students trying to escape had diminished to a mere trickle.

Lugh dropped into silence. As they got closer to the gym, he could feel the magic lingering there. With the Halloween decorations in the hall, the place feel a little scary, particularly since he knew they were stalking a woman who was using a strange form of magic.

The hairs on his arms rose and he realized how much energy Catherine was calling to her. It was vastly more than what he and Abby had used the night before. In the few seconds it took them to get to the gym, he wondered if in the training he'd been doing, he'd really seen the raw power his aunt could wield. He was so new to being a Magi, he had no idea what they were really capable of, other than moving down the Paths, making shields, and throwing energy around like he and Abby had. He slowed just enough to let Catherine take the lead as they stepped up to the gym doors.

Catherine paused with her fingers on the door handle. There was a big cardboard spider hanging on the window, making it impossible to see into the large room.

"She's set something." Catherine cocked her head as if trying to listen to something beyond the door.

Lugh let his magical senses extend outward like he'd been taught. It was similar to the seeking spell Catherine had done in the office, but more passive. Lugh wasn't looking for anything exact, just testing the environment around him.

He blinked in surprise at the presence of a strong shield. To his knowledge there were only three people in school who could use magic: himself, Abby and Wyn. But the magic he felt didn't exactly feel like the woman he'd encountered at the store and on his sidewalk. He poked at the shield with his mind, and to his surprise, it poked back.

"What?" He skittered backward until his back hit the smooth wall across the hall.

The return probe didn't extend far enough to reach him across the hall.

"Someone's trying to make sure they know who's coming in," Catherine said softly. "Are you okay?"

Lugh nodded. "Yeah." He drew on his magic and let his mind slip into the place where he could easily synch with his ring. Linking with his ring helped him relax in preparation for using his magic. Even after a few months, magically reaching out to his ring was becoming reflex before he started working magic. He wasn't as angry as he'd been the previous night. It wasn't as hard to access his magic. He formed a shield around himself.

"Good." Catherine nodded. "Let's go in there and see what they've got set for us. Stay behind me."

"Okay." Lugh dashed across the hall and stood right behind Catherine. He didn't want to do anything that might jeopardize them. They had people counting on them to come home.

With a deep breath, Catherine opened the door.

A pulse of magic roared out of the doors as soon as Catherine had the door halfway opened. Catherine managed to get up a shield. Lugh wasn't aware it was possible to strengthen a shield that fast. The doors came off their hinges and flew past them, slamming into the wall Lugh had been against only moments before. The concussive force of the spell washed around Catherine's shield like a river spilling around a boulder.

Catherine frowned. "Definitely not a normal Magus spell."

"What is she?" Lugh whispered. "Can you beat her?"

Without answering, Catherine went into the gym. Lugh almost expected the doors to slam shut behind them, except that the doors were across the hall. He couldn't imagine Catherine's magic was going to be able to keep people from noticing something like that, not while she faced the woman standing in the middle of the gym.

The strange woman from the previous night stood defiantly in center court. Her hands were on her narrow hips and her painted lips were pulled back in a scowl. "Oh, look, I got one of the mommas on my hook. I was only trying for one of the little ones."

"Who are you and what do you want in Steamboat?" Catherine asked.

"Who I am isn't going to help you much, Ms. Ballor. Oh, yes, I know who you are. I think most of the magical community knows of Catherine Ballor and the hold she maintains on the paths in this area."

"I'm guardian on the paths, a lot of Magi are." Catherine sounded confused, but she continued to draw power.

"Not as many as there used to be," the woman continued. "And when the guardians fall, the rest of us find easy ways to get around." She gestured and a massive ball of fire shot out toward them.

With a series of gestures that gave Lugh goosebumps, Catherine caught the fireball on her shield and sent it back at the woman. It was so hot, it warped the boards of the gym. Above them, the sprinkler system went off, sending gallons of water pouring down toward them. The shield Catherine had up blocked the water, which drenched the gym, doing further damage to the floors.

The woman caught the returning spell with outstretched hands and the flames died away. "Okay, so fire doesn't work on you. Looks like you're blocking water too. How well do you handle earth?" She gestured again, the motion looked like no rune Lugh had seen yet.

The school shook.

Lugh had never been in an earthquake, but he didn't doubt that was what was happening. The floor under him rolled. It made his stomach knot as he tried to stay on his feet.

"What's happening?" Bran shouted as Lugh's phone beeped with an incoming message.

"She's using the elements," Lugh replied.

"Lugh hit her low as I hit her high," Catherine whispered as the ground continued to rumble. "We've got to stop her before she does too much damage to the school and the town."

"Okay." Like he'd done the previous night, Lugh drew energy and focused it on his ring. He hoped the woman was affected by Catherine's invisibility shield on him, like the teachers and office staff had been.

Catherine unleashed a lance of magic at her that made the combined efforts of Lugh and Abby look miniscule by comparison.

It shattered the woman's shields and caught her in the chest. She flew backward into the bleachers which were closed against the far wall.

Following his aunt's direction, Lugh didn't want to see if the woman got up, he sent a blast of his own.

She flinched when it struck, then she got to her feet.

"So you did bring one of the kids with you. I guess my plan did work." The woman stood in the wreckage of the bleachers. The earthquake stopped. "But it had to. This is the only high school in the area. They had to go here."

She gestured and magic roared across the room. The debris from the bleachers and floors flew around and quickly became splinters and larger, all bouncing off Catherine's shield.

"She's an elemental," Catherine growled. "It's one of the few types of magic that's comparable to ours. She's good too. But we can use elemental magic too. Lugh, we haven't covered this, but each element has a complimentary element and each one has a contrary element. With air, the contrary element is earth, the complimentary one is fire."

Lugh watched as Catherine made the rune for fire, and for a moment he wondered if she was about to try and travel to a fire path, but she pushed more magic through the rune than she would've needed to move to a path. The rune blazed white bright and shot out of their protection toward the elemental. When it hit her winds, it grew in brightness. The winds were fanning the flames, not extinguishing them.

The elemental did something and got a shield up, but she was visibly scared by the effort she had to exert to protect herself.

Outside Catherine's shield, the winds died and the pieces of wood, metal and plaster that had been flying around fell to the floor.

"You're as good as your reputation, Ms. Ballor." Across the gym, the woman bowed to Catherine. "I'll be seeing you again real soon." She vanished, like she had from Lugh's sidewalk.

Catherine frowned. "She can't have gone far, she didn't use a Path."

"So what did she do?" Lugh didn't know any other way to disappear like that except for accessing a Path.

"She teleported," Catherine looked around the gym. "The authorities will be here in a moment, we need to be gone. Let's get back to the car and hope they haven't closed off the parking lot already. At least this didn't happen when school was in session."

Lugh could only nod as he followed Catherine out of the school. If all the students had been in class when the elemental attacked, there could've been people killed. As they raced down the halls, lockers were broken open, lights hung from odd angles, holiday decorations littered the floors as did text books and school papers. Somehow Lugh doubted they'd be having school the next day.

17

Which Witch is Which?

Lugh felt trapped. He desperately wanted to be helping in the search for the elemental witch who was attacking them, but Catherine had declared he, Abby and Wyn had to stay at his house with Bryan and one of the coven members watching them while she went in search of answers.

"Will you stop pacing?" Wyn asked, catching Lugh in a hug. "You're starting to make me nuts." He gave Lugh a quick kiss. "There's not much we can do so you might as well relax."

Abby sighed dramatically and turned from Lugh's computer. "He's got a point. They've all gone over-protective adult on us, so unless something major happens we're going to be out of the loop for a while. It'd be so nice if they'd actually accept the idea that we have a right to try to help. I mean Mom's magical backup is limited unless she can get ahold of Henry, Mark, or one of the other close-by Magi."

Lugh returned Wyn's kiss before taking his hand and going over to the bed. "Okay, so let's say she can't get them, does that give us a chance to get back in the fight?"

"Maybe." Abby shrugged. "To tell the truth, I was surprised when she took you with her to the school. But that was before she knew we're dealing with an Elemental witch here."

"Can you explain that a bit for me?" Lugh was getting really tired of having to ask a lot of questions every time something new popped up. He kept hoping that the learning curve for being a Magus would level out, but it stayed as steep as ever.

"Her power comes from the elements." Abby clicked into her common educated tone. At least when she used it, Lugh knew she wasn't going to elaborate much. "I know you know the four elements."

"You know some folks feel there are six elements," Wyn pipped up as he lay down next to Lugh and put his head in Lugh's lap. It was very similar to the way Bran would often curl up for cuddles.

Abby sighed. "I've heard about that, but there's really no evidence for the other two."

Lugh held up a hand before she went charging down the idea that Wyn was wrong. "What are the other two? I know about Earth, Air, Fire, and Water."

"Spirit and Time," Wyn said. "Although I've never understood how spirit can be an element."

"Exactly," Abby said. "Spirit is what we all are, outside of our physical bodies, it can't be an element, although some people look on it as a god power. It's not where we get our power from."

"What about time?" Lugh asked.

"What about it?" Abby sounded a bit condescending, like an adult might sound with a child who asked about something they weren't old enough to understand.

"Couldn't it be an element?" Lugh combed his hand through Wyn's hair, enjoying the way the silky blond locks played through his fingers.

"A lot of people think time is definitely as much an element as the prime four," Wyn said before Abby could. "It's something we're all immersed in from the moment we're conceived. There's no way to escape it. We can't survive without time, so why wouldn't it be an element?"

"But we can't control it like we can the prime four," Abby said. "That's what makes them more important."

Lugh had learned a bit about the four elements over the past few months. Each one had paths that could be walked. It wasn't until they'd faced the Elemental witch that he'd actually thought about trying to use their energy for magic. "So Magi can control the elements like that Elemental witch was doing?"

Abby nodded. "Yes. A lot of people find elemental manipulation fairly easy. Mom's not big into it. She thinks we can accomplish just as much using our personal energy and simply use nature and the elements to help recharge. She also thinks our way is a lot more precise. The difference between using a bullet and a cannon ball."

"I can see that comparison," Wyn said. "With a well-placed spell you can make an almost surgical strike, but throw the wrong kind of power around and you're basically hoping your target gets hit with the collateral damage."

"Not that your spells do much in the way of damage," Abby snapped and started to turn back around to Lugh's computer.

"Wait a sec." Lugh drew her attention back to him. "So are there other kinds of magic users out there too? I've only known about Magus and Wiccans before, now we've got Elemental. If there's more, it would be nice to be prepared for some of them."

"I could answer some of these questions," Bran said from the window ledge where he and Morrigan curled on the special cat perch Lugh and Wyn had installed a few weeks earlier to give Bran another spot to get more sun, which he complained he never got enough of.

"I'm sure you could, but this is helping to distract Abby," Lugh replied as he continued to stroke Wyn's hair.

"Well, there are actually a fair number of them. And they all have a dark side and a light side," Abby returned to her lecture tone. "We would first have to start by sorting out magic by the source of the power. There's a lot of different religious mystics out there. Some Wiccans are just religious and don't do any magic that doesn't help them worship their gods."

"And some are like my family and believe magic has a place in our everyday lives." Wyn caught Lugh's hand and kissed his fingers. The action sent little sparks of energy through Lugh and made him smile.

"Right," Abby agreed, then spun the computer chair around. "It's one of the reasons I can put up with you so well. You're just a little away from being a Magus. If you had a familiar, you might be one of us. But, anyway, when we move away from the religious folks, there are a number of different magic users. High magic folks without familiars are the closest to what we are. They use their magic in their daily lives and can be pretty impressive with it. Some of them incorporate any other magic system they can into their work. It makes them very versatile, but if a particular kind of magic is called for, it limits them."

She sighed and spun the chair again, making her hair stream out behind her. "You already know about Elemental witches. They normally specialize, having one element they are particularly attuned to."

Lugh nodded. "And your mom said this one is a bigger problem because she can use all four." He shivered. "I hope she can't use time too."

"Right." Wyn let go of Lugh's hand. "She did enough damage with just the prime four."

"At least the authorities are saying the quake ruptured a gas line and that's what caused all the damage." Lugh was always amazed at how the human mind quickly found a rational explanation for times when magic was used, even when the solution they came up with didn't fit all the facts. They'd done a little checking and the quake had been the worst to hit the area in over a hundred years. Steamboat Springs wasn't known for quakes, or tornadoes.

"Anyway, back to the kinds of magic." Abby made them all focus. "We've also got Necromancers; they draw their power from the dead."

"And raise zombies and such," Wyn added. "A lot of voodoo practitioners combine necromancy with their religious practices."

Abby frowned at him. "Who's explaining things to Lugh?"

Wyn put his arm around Lugh's leg as if being protective. "I thought we both were."

She shook her head. "Whatever. I bet you don't know about Plane Walkers."

"Plane Walkers?" Wyn turned toward her. "What are those? You're not just making that up are you?"

"Nope." Her tone went from lecture to superior. "But there aren't a lot of them around. Plane Walkers can draw power from other worldly sources and can move from one reality to another."

"Wait a minute." Lugh was hit with another new idea. "There's more than one reality?"

Abby nodded. "According to Mom, there's a lot of them. We're not normally concerned with them since we focus all our energy here on this plane. There might even be a plane out there where you weren't raised to be normal. There might be one where Wyn is a genius."

"Or there might be one where my dad is still alive." Lugh was never more than a thought or two from wanting to find a way to bring his dad back to life. He missed him so much.

"Probably," Abby agreed. "But unless a Plane Walker comes looking for help, or causes a problem, Mom always says to not worry about what's out beyond our world. There's enough problems here not to looking to other worlds for new and interesting ones."

"Catherine's back," Bran announced as he bounded off the perch and headed for the door.

Lugh pushed on Wyn to sit up. "Let's go see what Catherine found." He wanted to know what was going one, and hoped it was something they could help with. He didn't like sitting on the sidelines waiting for the action to continue.

18

Sketches and Leads

Catherine didn't look happy when they reached the kitchen. She paced around as Lugh's mom worked on dinner.

"Did you find anything?" Lugh asked before Abby could.

"Yes," Catherine didn't sound any more pleased than she looked. "I had to make more than a few calls, but I now know who we're dealing with."

"And who is she?" Abby blurted out. In recent months it had almost become a challenge between her and Lugh who could speak first. "Where's she from?"

"She's from California, outside of LA." Catherine stopped pacing and leaned up against the refrigerator. "She was part of a small Elemental coven out there. They had a problem with inside fighting and broke up about six months ago. Some of them were recruited by a group of Shadow Magi." She sighed and ran a hand through her graying red hair. "It looks like there's a growing number of forces working against the light. I guess we're more isolated here in Steamboat than I realized. I thought since we're on one of the major east-west paths I'd be kept apprised of what's going on in the world. I haven't been."

"What are you talking about?" Lugh's mom asked as she stirred a slowly simmering pot of spaghetti sauce, or at least that's what it smelled like to Lugh.

"The number of light workers has dropped significantly over the past year. Mostly through attacks from the shadows." Catherine shook her head. "I should've known. We'd be better prepared."

Lugh wanted to pace too, but Wyn caught his hand and pulled him down into one of the chairs at the table. "Does this mean that Dad might not have died in an accident? If the shadows are striking at the light, then there is a good chance, right?"

Catherine shrugged. "We may never know for sure. I don't like coincidence, but it is a possibility. Maybe if I can find the coven from Florida, I might learn more, but right now we need to focus on the immediate threat."

"Right." Abby nodded as she joined Lugh and Wyn at the table. "So what's her name? Names have power. We might be able to find her just with her name and stop her before she can attack us again."

Slowly, Lugh nodded. He liked the idea of taking the fight to the strange woman. It would be a lot better than sitting around guessing at what was happening.

"Sally," Catherine said. "Her name is Sally Gartin."

A soft chuckle came from Lugh's mom. "Not the name you would expect from an evil witch trying to kill you kids."

"No, it's not," Catherine agreed. "But I doubt her mother would've named her Lady Shadow."

"I like that, can we call her that?" Abby blurted out with a lot more enthusiasm than Lugh thought the situation warranted. "Lady Shadow."

"Abby, I don't know if that's a good idea," Lugh's mom said as she went and got a pile of plates.

"Actually, it might not be a bad idea," Catherine countered, and pointed at Abby. "There are some powerful magic users who can tell when their name is used. If we have an alias for her that only we know, we can use it and if she's listening for her name, she won't be any the wiser."

Abby grinned. "Cool. I got to name our first major bad guy, or girl in this case."

"But this doesn't help us find her," Bryan spoke up. "That's what we need to do. Find her and convince her she needs to leave us alone."

"But a name does help us find her," Catherine said. "Now with that, I can scry for her around the city. If she's anywhere in the Steamboat area, I can find her."

"I can have the coven out checking around. We should be able to put together a good drawing on her," Bryan suggested. "Maybe between all our efforts we can get the drop on her."

Wyn laughed. "Dad, you sound like a cop on TV now. I don't think they really say 'get the drop on people.'"

"Then we should bring back that term. It's fairly useful, I think." He walked over and ruffled Wyn's hair.

Wyn cringed. "Dad, I wish you wouldn't do that."

Bryan chuckled and ruffled Wyn's hair again. "Wyn, I'll probably do that do you until you don't have any hair. It's a father's prerogative."

Crossing his arms, Wyn frowned at his father but didn't say anything.

Lugh always wished his own father was still around when he saw Wyn and his father interacting. It gave him a huge lump in his throat and a tightness in his chest. He kept hoping the reaction would get easier with time, but so far it hadn't.

"Anyway," Catherine drew their attention back to her. "I called one of the local artists to come over and work with Lugh, Abby and me to get a sketch of Sal…Lady Shadow. Once we have that. I'll use it and her name to scry for her, and we can get the coven out working on combing the streets. With any luck, we'll have her located by morning."

"At least we don't have to worry about school tomorrow," Wyn said, still frowning in his father's direction.

"Don't expect that to last," Lugh's mom said as she drained the pasta. "I'm sure the school board is already working on somewhere for you kids to keep up your classes."

"Hey, maybe it will be an online thing where we don't actually have to go to school, just show up in cyber class at the appointed time," Lugh suggested. The idea of not actually having to go to physical school was an uplifting one. He could handle just doing his classes from the computer.

"I doubt it," Catherine said. "Steamboat isn't that advanced yet. That would take more time to set up than it will take to repair the school."

"Oh." Lugh did his best not to pout. It was a good idea.

"At least then we could be together all day instead of me having to stay at the shop," Bran pipped up.

That was an angle Lugh hadn't even thought of.

"Alright, let's everyone eat," Lugh's mom said. "Grab a plate and a fork, then serve yourself." She pulled a cookie sheet out of the oven with cheesy garlic bread on it and set it on the stove next to the pasta and sauce.

It didn't take long for all the food she'd made to disappear. Lugh was always hungry after doing magic, and lately he'd been eating more than ever; he felt like a bottomless pit, but he wasn't putting on weight, so he didn't worry about it. Catherine had said something about magic burning calories the same as exercise. That was also why magic made him tired.

Before they were finished with dinner, the artist Catherine had asked to come over was there, and Lugh managed to get out of helping Abby and Wyn with the dishes to give her his description of Lady Shadow. The woman explained how she occasionally worked with the police to help them with suspect sketches, but she mostly did caricatures of tourists. She took each of their descriptions separately and compiled their accounts of her features to make a single picture. Lugh was surprised at how accurate the picture was when it was done. He hoped it would be enough to catch the woman and stop her from causing problems so they could get back to figuring out what had happened to Espe and help the spirit Magus find the rest she deserved.

19

Off into the Night

"Lugh, wake up." Bran pushed against Lugh's head. *"Come on."*

Lugh opened his eyes and stared into the cat's face. "What? It's still dark outside."

"Exactly." Bran sat back and tilted his head. *"Nighttime is the perfect time to prowl around and find what we're looking for."*

"No." Lugh yawned and rolled away from Bran. "Mom and Aunt Catherine would both kill us if we went out to find either Lady Shadow or Espe by ourselves."

"Which is why Morrigan and I are going too," Abby said from somewhere in the darkness.

Lugh frantically made sure he didn't have anything sticking out from his covers. "What are you doing in here?" He fumbled with the lamp on his bedside table.

Abby huffed as she walked over and sat on the bed. Morrigan jumped up beside Bran. "Trying to make sure Bran gets you awake so we can go talk to Espe. She only shows up at night. I don't plan to take on Lady Shadow on our own. You're right—our moms would kill us, but Espe isn't a threat to us. We just need to figure out what she needs and how to help her. With Mom focused on the more pressing matter of the Elemental witch, we've got to help Espe before Samhain passes."

"But that's still a couple days away," Lugh stifled another yawn and was more thankful than ever they didn't have to worry about school the next morning.

"Right, but it's not like someone throws a switch at midnight on Samhain and the veil is suddenly thin." Abby shook her head. "This whole season the veil slowly thins, then slowly thickens again. We have a few days before it's at its thinnest, but it's already heading that direction. If we can help Espe, that'll make things easier for Mom."

Lugh really wished she'd leave his room. He didn't see any point in trying to argue with her. If there was one thing he learned very quickly after meeting his cousin, it was that it didn't pay to try to argue with her on most things. She was just too pigheaded. But he'd like to get dressed without her there.

She frowned in his direction. "So are you going to get up so we can do this, or not?"

"Are you going to leave me alone so I can do it?" he responded. He was really beginning to think the idea of the two of them staying close together to make it easier for Catherine to protect them both from Lady Shadow was a bad idea. It was giving Abby way too much access to him.

"Boys." She cocked her head and glared at him, then got off the bed. "Come on Morrigan. Let's give Lugh some privacy. We'll meet him and Bran on the front porch in five minutes."

"Grab me a power bar and a bottle of water, please." Lugh waited but she didn't respond before she slipped out of the room and closed the door. Somehow he figured if they hadn't been trying to be quiet, she probably would've slammed the door behind her. She wasn't prone to doing things just because he wanted her to do them.

"This is going to be great." Bran jumped from the bed onto Lugh's dresser. It always looked like he was trying to be careful and not scatter things when he was up on places like the dresser. It was one of the many things that set him apart from regular cats.

Lugh sighed as he slipped out from his bed. "We'll see." After a couple of nighttime adventures with Bran, he'd grown suspicious as to who was supposed to be having the fun, he or his familiar. Of course they'd never had Abby and Morrigan along on one yet. But somehow that didn't make Lugh feel any more confident that things were going to go smoothly.

Abby threw the power bar at him as he quietly opened the front door.

Lugh somehow managed to not slam the screen door and catch the bar at the same time. He stared at the foil-wrapped bar for a moment. When he'd first bonded to Bran, there had been a minor discussion about how he and Bran would become more alike over time. He'd always figured he'd start having the urge to chase birds and squirrels or something, but if it was going to improve his reflexes, he might get to like it…a lot.

"Took you long enough," Abby snapped.

"Sorry. Had to find clean socks." Lugh unwrapped the bar. "Mom's been busy lately and hasn't done laundry." He always hated how hard his mother worked to make sure they had enough money to get by. He wished he was old enough to get a job and help out.

"If there's nothing cool going on tomorrow, maybe we can do it for her," Abby said, then opened her own bar. "Okay. The last place we saw Espe was here on the walk."

"Right." Lugh nodded. At least Abby wasn't suggesting they go traipsing all over town looking for the ghost.

"So we start here and see if we can contact her."

"And how do we do that exactly?" Lugh thought they needed a bunch of candles and a crystal ball or Ouija board for that, and it didn't look like Abby had anything of the sort.

"We're going to meditate." Abby finished off her bar, wadded up the foil package and slipped it into her pocket.

Meditating was one of Lugh's least favorite parts of magic. Sure it helped him get his thoughts in order for doing magic, but beyond that, he always thought it was kinda boring.

"Morrigan and I will make sure nothing happens to you while you meditate," Bran said as he walked down the street.

"Thanks," Lugh muttered. "I thought that was just one of the things familiars were supposed to do for their humans."

Abby giggled. "You know, you're kinda grumpy when you get woken up in the middle of the night. You better get used to it. Magical emergencies don't keep banker's hours. Or at least that's what Mom says." She sat down just off the walkway, almost exactly where they'd seen Espe the previous night. Once she was settled, she looked up at Lugh, then patted the walk in front of her.

Trying not to grumble anymore, Lugh strolled over and sat down. The concrete under his butt was colder than he expected and he immediately wished he was sitting next to Abby on the dead leaves. "Okay, now what?"

"Now we let our minds drift and see if we can find any hint of Espe." Abby closed her eyes and took a deep breath.

Lugh half figured he'd be back to sleep in a couple of minutes, even on the cold walk way. He followed her example and did as Aunt Catherine had taught him. Letting his mind relax and feeling the world around him. Abby was a shining column of magic in front of him. Her glow was a lot different from Espe's aura. It was one of the first auras Lugh had ever seen. It was familiar and almost comforting, not that he'd admit that to Abby. With each breath, Lugh relaxed a little more. He felt like he was about to fall asleep, when Bran spoke in his head.

"Lugh, something's happening."

It took a lot of control for Lugh to not jerk and break the relaxed state he'd achieved. *"What?"* He didn't want to speak aloud and risk breaking Abby's mediation.

"Feels like Espe's coming."

Lugh slowly opened his eyes. His front yard was awash in soft bluish hues. It reminded him of the blue light that normally surrounded Espe. It was a lot different from the gray world of the paths he could walk as a Magus. It seemed colder than the paths, and that was saying something because when he'd stepped off the paths it got downright frigid.

Trying to maintain his meditative mind, Lugh moved slowly, turning his head to get a look around. Everything had the same bluish glow to it, everything except Abby who still glowed with the Magus magic he'd seen before.

Abby's eyes were open. "I think she's here."

Lugh nodded. He wasn't sure he wanted to talk just yet, afraid of breaking the delicate web they seemed to have entered.

"You came." Espe materialize between Lugh and Abby. "I wasn't sure you would." Beside her, the cocker spaniel sat and began licking its paw.

"Espe, we want to help you," Lugh said.

Espe looked around. "It is fairly lonely here."

"Right, and you don't deserve to be lonely anymore." Lugh had no idea what to say, or even what information they wanted to get out of Espe.

"Where are you exactly?" Abby said, and for once, Lugh was thankful she was always so quick to speak up.

Espe looked around. Lines of confusion wrinkled her brow. "I don't really know. I'm pretty sure we're still in Colorado. I know I walked a long way after I felt Colin…but you aren't really Colin are you?"

Lugh shook his head. "Colin was my dad."

"Was"— Espe frowned—"What happened?"

"He and his familiar were killed in a boating accident." Lugh hated talking about what happened to his dad, and since coming to Steamboat, he'd done it a lot more than he had ever thought he would.

"When I knew him, he was a good boy… The best." Espe looked at Abby, as if seeing her for the first time. "Are you Catherine's daughter then?"

Abby nodded. "Abby. And that is Lugh, since he hasn't bothered to introduce himself.

Espe smiled. "Like the god."

"Right," Lugh replied. "Espe, what happened to you?"

She sighed and stared at her feet. "I don't exactly know. I was attacked on the path that runs from Colorado Springs to Woodland Park. I was going up there to see my grandmother. He was more powerful than I was, but I don't know who he was, other than he was a Magus."

"What kind of familiar did he have?" Abby asked. "We might be able to talk to other Magi who were around at the time to figure out who it was."

"He had a ferret." She rubbed her dog's head. "Carmine kept trying to get at it as we fought, but it stayed in his pocket the whole time. She's been blaming herself, saying if she'd been able to get to the ferret, maybe I could've bested the Magus."

"Did he enter the path with you?" Abby looked like she didn't believe the story.

Espe shook her head. "He was waiting for me. I don't know how he managed to be in the same phase as I was, but he did. I've never heard of anything like that before."

"Then he killed you on the path?" Lugh began to wonder if the Shadow Magus he fought off the paths had suffered the same fate as Espe and might still be out there somewhere, a glowing shade of himself. He shuddered. He didn't like the idea of thinking that he could've caused someone to suffer a fate worse than death.

"Yes." Espe turned her head and for the first time, dark bruises were visible on her neck. "And when I was gone, Carmine had no choice but to follow. That is the sad fate of our familiars." Carmine rubbed up against Espe's leg, almost cat-like.

"Do you know how we can help you find peace?" Lugh desperately wanted to find a way to help Espe. They might not be able to do much on the Lady Shadow front, but helping Espe find the solace she deserved would make him feel better.

"I don't know." Espe frowned again. "Since I died, I've spent my time helping other Magi in need. When I felt your power the other night, I had hoped you were Colin." She focused her attention on Lugh. Her ghostly blue gaze made him shiver. "You look so much like him."

"I get that a lot."

"Then you came to help us last night," Abby cut in, drawing Espe's gaze back to her. "Do you know why your attack was so much stronger than ours on Lady Shadow?"

Espe cocked her head. "That's a strange name for a witch. Why is she called Lady Shadow?"

Lugh couldn't help but chuckle. It made sense to him and Abby that they should give an alias to their foe, but back in time, Espe probably never would've dreamed about that. She probably didn't know much about superheroes and supervillains. "We call her that."

"That way we don't have to use her name," Abby blurted before Lugh could finish explaining.

"Hmmm." Espe nodded slightly. "It would also keep her from hearing when people say her name. It makes sense. To be truthful, I'm not exactly sure why my attack had more impact than yours. What I have discovered over the years of being a spirit, is that spirit magic, even if I do the same things I did when I was alive, often has a greater impact on the world around us. Maybe being a spirit revives my magical motor or something."

"Then I'll have to remember to stay out of your way." Lady Shadow appeared on the sidewalk a few feet away from them.

20

Different Frequencies

Lugh was on his feet, his quiet meditative feeling shot. From the porch, Bran yowled and Morrigan hissed. Abby's magic swirled around him as Espe's dog began to bark. The air was suddenly super charged.

"Don't you ever get tired?" Lugh asked while calling up a shield. After walking the paths, it was one of the first things Catherine had taught him.

"Elemental magic has its uses," Lady Shadow said. "We have the limitless power of the elements to draw from."

"But each element has its opposite," Abby said. Her magic blazed across the yard and struck the shield Lady Shadow erected.

Magical force illuminated the area as the conflicting magics collided.

Espe's bolt of magical force followed Abby's. It caused Lady Shadow to stumble backward.

A frown appeared on her face. "You're not supposed to get involved, you're a spirit. The world of the living means nothing to you."

"You're wrong." Espe stalked forward. "I might just be a spirit, but there are still good people in this world who need me, and I will protect them." Beside her, Frieda fell silent, then rushed Lady Shadow's shield.

In blurs of gray and black, Bran and Morrigan raced to follow Frieda in attacking the Elemental Witch's defenses.

Lugh didn't want to just watch. He had to help. She was standing on the walkway to his house. Lugh had discovered a small tread of an air path that ran from one of the large paths to his house. He'd never told his mother, but he'd used it more than once to slip out when he wanted to go somewhere he didn't want her knowing about, normally out to meet Wyn.

"Bran!" Lugh shouted as he moved to stand in the path. He knew he could access the path without his familiar, he'd done it before, but he also knew it was easier and safer for him to be in contact with Bran when he accessed the magical routes Magus used to move around faster than normal humans.

Bran broke off his attack and leapt for Lugh, landing in his arms. *What are we going to do?*

"See if we can get through her shields." Lugh drew the rune for an air path and pushed the power out to the path. He'd struggled at first to learn to walk the paths, but it was easier than it had been. He'd been practicing. Making it to an air path had become almost second nature. He was in perfect synch with his ring and Bran. The power answered his call and they slipped into the path.

The gray world of the air paths encompassed him. It was a strange overlay of the real world. The hues were muted and dulled. Lady Shadow was still standing in the walkway. Her shield was a bright light in the gray.

Lugh dashed forward. The shield stopped him.

He shook his head. "This doesn't make sense. I could get through the shields of the Shadow Magi."

"She's different than they are," Bran scrambled up on Lugh's shoulder. *"Her power comes from the elements. We have to work on different frequencies. Our power is stronger here. We just have to find the right frequencies to slip through her shields."*

A few months earlier, he wouldn't have understood, but with his training, he did. Lugh focused on his ring. He knew different elements operated at different frequencies. It didn't take much for him to see the vibrations the shield functioned at. It was a lower pulse rate than the air magic he'd seen before.

"Earth?" Lugh asked.

"Looks that way," Bran agreed.

Lugh knew how to work with air. He channeled the higher frequency down the path and into his ring. Being on the air path made it easy. He sent a blast of air into the earth shield.

"What's going on!" Lady Shadow shrieked.

Focusing more power from the path through his ring, Lugh made a lance of force and hit the shield again. Lady Shadow's shield crumbled in a shower of bright colored sparks. Something surged along the path.

"What is that?" Bran and Lugh shouted together.

The path quaked. Everything shimmered with brown and red power. The gray world of the path fell away, and Lugh and Bran were on the walk in front of his house again, but they were up against the spot where Lady Shadow's had been. But it was gone, as was she.

"You drove her off!" Abby shouted and hugged Lugh.

"What?" Lugh stared at her as he slowly returned the hug.

"You drove her off." Abby let go of him. "Whatever you did, you made her leave."

"How did she make me fall off the path?" Lugh still felt odd. The strange surge from the path made his head hurt. It had to be something Lady Shadow did.

Abby stared at him. "She just disappeared."

"There's something about her power that impacts our magics," Espe said. "She's more than just an elemental witch. That extra something is what makes her more dangerous."

It was something different that Lugh hadn't heard about. "What is it?"

"Lugh!" His mother raced out of the house. "What happened?" She stopped and stared at Espe. "Who is she?"

"Mom, this is Espe, the spirit Magus we've been talking about." Lugh hoped his mother would understand and not freak out.

"Abby, are you okay?" Catherine followed Lugh's mom out of the house.

"Fine, Mom," Abby replied.

Catherine hugged Abby, before turning to Espe. "You haven't changed much, Espe, other than this plane of existence isn't your natural plane anymore, is it?"

Espe frowned. "You have changed, Catherine. I also understand that Colin is no longer among the living."

"Right," Catherine replied with a dark look. "We need to talk so we can make plans."

"Don't you think we need to track Lady Shadow and take this fight to her?" Lugh was tired of just reacting to her attacks. It wasn't right that they spent a lot of time talking about things and waited for the bad guys to come to them.

"We have to know more about her," Catherine replied. "I think she's some kind of psychic in addition to being an Elemental. That's how she keeps disappearing."

"She's teleporting, not using the paths," Abby added.

"I think so," Catherine said.

"So what does that mean?" Lugh's mom asked. "That she can appear anywhere?"

"Not exactly, but close," Catherine replied.

"We aren't safe, are we?" his mom asked.

Catherine shook her head. "Not from a teleporter. Margaret, let's face it. We're living in a turbulent time when the forces of darkness are trying to obliterate the forces of light. They're trying to upset the very balance of nature. We are all going to be pushed to the limits of our endurance and more. There isn't anywhere you can run. We're going to have to face this head on, even the things like Lady Shadow that we don't totally understand."

"Then I have to agree with Lugh, you need to take this fight to her." Lugh's mom hugged him. "I never wanted this for you."

He hugged her back. "I know Mom, but we can't go back now."

"She's being calmer than normal." Bran rubbed against Lugh's mother's arm.

Lugh didn't bother responding. He was as amazed as Bran at how well his mother was taking everything. He expected her to be trying to load him up and take him somewhere far away from magic. Something had changed. He wanted to know, but they didn't have time to talk about it.

"We should go inside," Catherine said. She looked at Espe. "Are you going to disappear again, or will you stay and talk?"

"I think we should stay." Espe looked at her dog. "There's nothing for us to go do right now. It feels like the right thing to do."

Lugh's mother took his hand. "I think she's right, we should go inside before the neighbors start to talk."

With familiars in tow, they hurried back inside. Lugh wondered when the next time Lady Shadow was going to show up and cause them problems. He just hoped they'd be more ready than they had been the past few times it had happened.

21

Espe's Tale

Lugh had no clue what they were supposed to do once they got into the house. He stayed next to his mother as they went into the living room. As they all took seats he realized they'd gotten into the habit of sitting in the same seats every time he, his mother, Abby and Catherine sat in the living room. Abby and Catherine took the couch and he and his mother took their favorite chairs.

Espe looked out of place, pacing around the open space around the coffee table.

"How did you die?" Catherine cut to the chase.

"I don't exactly know." Espe stared at her hands. "I was on the path going up into the mountains. I was going up to visit my grandmother. Someone met me on the path. I couldn't make out a face. They had on a hoodie."

"But they attacked you on the path?" Catherine asked. "He, or she would've had to enter the path with you."

"But they didn't," Espe said. "Freida and I entered the path from the tiny path near my parents' house, like we normally did."

"So how could they interact with you on the path then?" Lugh wondered out loud. He'd been told since he learned to walk the paths that the only way two people could interact on the paths is if they entered together. He'd seen other people on the paths before, but he'd only been able to interact with someone he'd come onto the path with.

Espe shook her head. "I don't really know. It all happened so fast. One minute we were trotting along, I think we were almost to Woodland Park, then the person who killed me appeared. They were blocking my way. I stopped because they looked too clear, too solid, like someone I'd see in the real world if we were both walking down the same trail in the forest."

Catherine stroked Bast and a thoughtful line crossed her forehead. "I've heard of it before, but the person has to be deliberately trying to get on the same path as someone else."

"So it might've been a Magus?" Lugh's mother asked.

"No." Catherine shook her head. "That's not how Magus magic works. Some of the other magics can cross over to ours. We're not the only ones who can use the paths. Each kind of magic user has their own way of crafting energies. I'll need to check and see what I can find out, but it might take a while."

"Why are we worrying about this in the past when there's a real danger to all of us right now?" Lugh's mother sounded very tired.

Catherine rubbed her nose. "I think there might be something tied into both situations. If there is any kind of organized group working against us, we need to know about it. We need to figure out what's driving the darkness into attacking us. If it's been building for twenty-five years, we need to know that. If it's something that's focused on a particular school of magic, we need to know."

"But how is that possible?" Lugh asked. "The Shadow Magi weren't Elementals, were they?" He'd been trying to understand everything, but there was so much flying at him. His mind was muddled and confused. It was one thing when there was a coven of Shadow Magi stealing magical items and killing familiars in an attempt to weaken Catherine and the other light workers in the area, but dealing with an Elemental Witch going after them and learning there was so many different ways of doing magic made his head spin. He wanted to understand everything he possibly could, but sometimes learning about magic was as confusing as English class in school. He always wanted to make sure he had his punctuation just right.

"No," Catherine replied quickly. "There was nothing about them that felt like Elemental magic. They were using Magi magic, pure and simple."

"I guess it'd be too simple to find a link that easily," Lugh said. The one thing he did know about magic was things were never simple and easy. Everything had to be just perfect to make things work right.

"Right." Catherine stopped petting Bast as the cat jumped down onto the floor. "But that doesn't mean there aren't links between them and Lady Shadow."

"And how do we find those?" Lugh asked.

"In the past, we'd spend lots of time trying to locate their teachers and such," Catherine said. "We'll have to go hit the internet. I can make some phone calls. We never found out the names of the Shadow Magi who attacked this summer. But we do have Sally's name. That's a starting point. We've already gotten some information. We'll do some more digging. See if we can find a connection."

"At least internet stuff is things you'll let us help with," Abby said.

"It helps to keep you both out of trouble." Catherine gave Abby a quick side hug. "But right now, I'd like to get a little more info from Espe." Her gaze traveled to the spirit Magus. "Do you know why you didn't move on?"

Espe shook her head. "When I was killed, I drifted for a while almost like someone who is lost off the paths. But I found my way back to the path. I don't know how long it took me. Time runs funny for spirits. There's a lot to distract us."

"I've heard that." Catherine patted her lap right before Bast jumped back up there. "When did you actually make it back to the real world long term?"

"A few months ago." Espe sat on the floor, and her dog hoped in her lap. "Before that, I'd come and go as Magi needed help. I realize now, that it might've been Colin's passing that called me back. Gave me the focus to get where I needed to be." She looked at Lugh. "I think I need to be here to keep Lugh safe."

"You don't need her, you have me," Bran said. *"Familiars always keep their Magi safe."*

Lugh rubbed Bran's head, but didn't respond.

"Why does Lugh need to be kept safe?" his mother asked reaching across the space between their chairs to touch his hand.

"Can't you see?" Espe glanced at her. "There are forces working against us. We have to protect our children. Maybe it was a spell Colin cast as he passed that called me back. That might've been what drew me to Lugh."

Catherine nodded as she stroked Bast. "That would make sense, but it would've had to be something Colin cast before he died, long before. There are spells out there to summon spirit guardians. If he cast one, and set it to trigger if something happened to him, that might explain why Espe showed up. But that doesn't exactly explain why it was Espe who was called."

"Maybe he knew I was dead and would be willing to protect his son," Espe said. "I was confused at first, but things are making a lot more sense now. The more I'm around Lugh and the rest of you, the clearer things become."

"We can hope that's the case," Catherine said. "I can't see Colin doing something like binding you without your permission." She pursed her lips and shook her head.

"At least if this is the case, Colin was looking out for Lugh," his mother said.

"Right." Lugh had always expected his father and mother to both be there to watch over him. Knowing his father had taken precautions to make sure he was taken care of made him feel a lot better about things, but didn't take away the lingering sting of his father's death.

"We'll never know for sure what Colin did before or after he died," Catherine said. "All we can know is what has happened since."

"If we could go back to where he died, we might be able to find out what happened to him," Espe said.

"We can't do that," Catherine said before Lugh or his mother had a chance to but in. "It happened at sea. There was an accident."

Espe sighed and shook her head. "The sea water would've dispersed the magic. There won't be any trace left behind. That's sad."

Catherine straightened. "I hadn't stopped to think about that before. If Colin was attacked with magic on the sea, it wouldn't leave any trace." She rubbed her chin thoughtfully. "It *might* be tied into what else is going on."

"More evidence that magic is bad for my family," Lugh's mother said.

"Keep reminding yourself that magic is not all goodness and light," Catherine said. "But you don't have to face them alone. We're all in this together. Colin might still be alive if he'd had family nearby."

Lugh's mother glared at her. "We wanted our own life."

"Mom." Lugh patted her arm. "Don't worry about the past. We have to worry about now. We've got to keep it together and work to get out of this."

She turned toward him and took his hand in hers. She was shaking hard, a sure sign of her stress levels. "I know. But sometimes, it's all just a bit too much. That's why your father and I left Colorado. To get him away from everyone. To give us a chance at a real life. We knew we'd have kids one day and wanted you to have every chance to be normal. This isn't normal. You deserve better. If I hadn't gotten the job offer here, we wouldn't have come back."

"I know Mom, but this is our life and we have to do what we can to stay alive." They'd had this conversation before. In the past few months, he'd begun to wonder how many times his mother and father had this same conversation about safety. He understood she was not magical and their world of paths, powers and familiars was scary to her. Recently she'd begun to soften on her stance, but suddenly it was like all her fears were coming back. He didn't want to have to go back to her worrying about everything he did.

Catherine stood, holding Bast to her chest. "It's been a long day, I think we should all retire for the night. We can make more plans in the morning."

"That's a good idea," Lugh's mom agreed. She rose from the chair and looked down at Lugh. "You go get some sleep."

"What if something happens?" Lugh wasn't sure he'd be able to get a good night's sleep, but had to admit they were both right. It had been a long day and he was more than a little bit tired. He'd used more magic than he was used to. He knew he needed the sleep, but just wasn't sure he'd be able to get it.

"Lady Shadow is going to be as tired as we are," Catherine said. "As long as she doesn't have an accomplice, we should be fine. She'll need rest."

"That sounds good," Lugh's mom said.

Bran yawned. *"I know I could definitely use a long nap."*

Lugh shook his head. "Okay. Let's get some sleep." He didn't like feeling as if he was giving up, but couldn't deny how tired he was. Magic would be easier if he had some rest. He scooped up Bran. The cat purred in his arms, then they headed off to bed after saying quick good nights.

22

Under the Bridge on the Path

Lugh did his best not to yawn. It hadn't taken the school long to set up a temporary location in the community center. Mr. Lester, his math teacher, was back to droning on about fractions and long equations. Lugh had spent several long nights trying to dig up more information about Lady Shadow, the Shadow Magi and more of the dark magic users. Even with him, Abby and Wyn doing everything they could, there wasn't much to go on. They didn't leave any obvious trails to be followed, either in the real world, or the internet. It had also been the longest Lady Shadow had gone without showing up since she first appeared in Steamboat Springs.

Halloween was just a day away, and in addition to trying to figure out everything they could about the dark forces working against them, they were sorting out what they were going to do with Espe. Since she was no longer just a random spirit, but someone who may have been called by his father to watch over him, Lugh didn't think it was right for them to talk about just dismissing her. The fact that she didn't want to be laid to rest, complicated things. Catherine was fairly adamant about not doing anything to send Espe to her eternal slumber if she was definitely coherent about what was going on around her and didn't want to go.

The community center's intercom system buzzed, a signal they'd all been waiting for. Not only was Lugh's math class done, but his school day was over. Since most of their classes were all in the once large room of the center, there wasn't any of the usual chaos of the kids all running down the hall for the front door, but there was a fair amount of cheering as the kids evacuated the building.

"Over here, Lugh!" Wyn shouted as soon as Lugh cleared the doors that dumped out onto the city park.

Lugh turned toward his voice and grinned. "Hey!" He waved and dashed to Wyn's side. They'd missed less than a week of school, and spent the entire time doing research, but he was ready to spend a few more days out of school and with Wyn all the time.

Wyn gave him a big hug. "This is going to get old fast, isn't it?"

"If by this, you mean school, not at school… Yeah, I think you're right there." Lugh took Wyn's hand and they started walking toward Catherine's shop; they were supposed to check in there before they did anything else. The way all the adults were spending extra time watching everything they did was beginning to chafe, but he understood. He was ready for the urgency of everything to be over and they could go back to just being regular kids again.

"Wait up!" Abby shouted as she sprinted across the park. "You two are sure taking off quickly."

Lugh nodded. "Needed to get out of the mob of people."

"Riiiight." Abby fell into step with them. "So, I have an idea."

"Good idea or bad idea?" Wyn asked.

Lugh chuckled, then ducked his head when she glared at him.

"Good idea," Abby snapped. "At least *I* think it's a good idea."

"We're in trouble now," Lugh said, unable to keep his mouth shut. But truthfully, if she'd come up with anything good, they needed to see what they could do with it. They were painfully at a dead end.

Abby put her hands on her hips. "If we're lucky we won't be. After we check in with Mom, we're going to head over to your house and make a stop on the way."

That got Lugh's attention. "Where are we going to stop? There's not a ton of places we can stop between the shop and my house."

"You'll see," Abby said with more than a little bit of attitude. "This is going to be cool."

Her enthusiasm made Lugh nervous. His cousin didn't get excited about things like normal girls did. If she was up to something, they could all end up in a lot of trouble. But if they were lucky, they might get some clues on what was going on.

"Okay, we're here," Abby announced. "We've got to be quick. If we take too long, our folks will figure out we're up to something."

"You still haven't told us exactly what we're doing." Lugh stared around the park. There were several bridges crossing some of the small streams that fed out into the Yampa River. A number of walking trails crossed the green grass; luckily, most of them were empty. The few flower beds around them were brown and dying in the autumn coolness.

"I think she's just being rude and delaying my dinner," Bran objected.

"I doubt that," Lugh said.

"Wait a minute." Wyn stopped just shy of stepping onto the bridge they were about to cross. "Are you about to tell me that the troll who's rumored to live under this bridge is real?"

"What?" Lugh looked between the two of them. "Troll? As in a fairy who lives under bridges and wants tolls for people walking over them? That kind of troll?" In all the magic he'd been exposed to, the closest thing they'd come to anything that wasn't human were the familiars who were still animals he recognized and had dealt with before learning about magic. The idea that there could be a troll living under a bridge in a park was way far beyond anything he'd even stopped to think about.

Abby stared at the two of them. "To Wyn, yes, sorta. To Lugh, yes. I really do wish the two of you would start coordinating your questions. Now, we don't have time to stand around here and debate this. Lugh, we need to walk the paths to get to her lair. If Wyn is coming with us, you get to bring him along. I'm going to want to keep my hands free."

"Do you want to come or stay here?" Lugh asked, just to make sure, although he was already pretty sure he knew the answer. Wyn didn't like being left out of their magical adventures when it was avoidable.

Wyn gave him his best "Duh" look but didn't say anything.

"Okay, I guess that settles it." Abby picked up Morrigan. "Lugh, follow me, we're going to the water path that runs along the stream here. Everyone take a deep breath."

Lugh touched Abby's shoulder as Bran hopped up on his. Then he took Wyn's hand. If Abby was going to open the path, all he had to do was stay in physical contact with her when she opened the path and again when she returned to the normal world. Since he'd never traveled a water path before, Lugh had no idea what to expect and did as he was told and took a deep breath.

"You remember I hate getting wet," Bran grumbled.

Abby had already begun drawing the rune for water, so Lugh couldn't verbalize his response. *"I hope it's just for a moment."* He had no idea how long they were going to be wet.

Power surged around them as Abby pushed energy out to open the way for them. It made the hair on Lugh's arms stand up and sent a shiver down his spine.

The water path opened to Abby's spell and she walked into it. The path wasn't the pale gray world of an air path, but was soft blues, and sure enough, it was wet. It was also colder than Lugh expected.

He ignored Bran's complaints as they slipped down the path, dropping below the bridge until Abby made another rune, the reverse of the one to get onto the path. Seconds later she pulled them into an underwater grotto that led into a cave.

Strange glowing crystals dotted the walls and provided them with enough light to see by.

"Wow, I did it." Abby beamed as she stepped out from under Lugh's hand.

"Wait a minute!" Wyn wiped his hand through his wet hair, pushing strands off his forehead. "Are you saying you've never been here before?"

Abby cocked her head and glared at him. "No, silly. I've been here before, but I've always come with Mom. It took a lot more to get here than I thought it would."

"And you do not have your mother's finesse, young Magus," a woman said from behind them.

As his heart raced, Lugh let go of Wyn's hand and spun toward the voice. He wished he could push Wyn behind him where he'd be easier to protect. He didn't like what he saw, it was a creature of nightmares.

23

Talking with the Troll

The creature was a green that reminded Lugh of fresh seaweed that had washed up on the beach in Florida. Her hair was a wash of tangled olive that looked like a ghillie suit one of his friend's father had back in Florida. Her eyes were huge and orange with no discernible pupils.

"Terrabeth, it's me, Abby," Abby said with a tremble in her voice.

"I remember you, Catherine Ballor's daughter." Her voice was the only part of her, beyond her basic shape, that was the least bit human. "Why have you come?"

Abby walked over to stand just a couple of feet from her. "We're working on something big and need to know if you've seen or felt anything."

Terrabeth frowned, or at least Lugh thought it was a frown. She had flabby jowls, much like an orangutan, if an orangutan was green instead of orange, and that made it hard for him to decide if she had frowned or had simply sighed. "With you Magi around, there's always something to sense, and of late, I stay here under my bridge, it's safer that way."

"So you haven't felt the Elemental witch who's come to town?" Abby pressed.

A deep furrow appeared across Terrabeth's forehead, at least that's what Lugh though it was. "The one who disrupts water, along with everything else?"

Abby beamed. "Yes, that's her."

Terrabeth shook her head and sat on the rocky ground of her grotto. It put her on eye level with Lugh. "So much magic that one throws around. It's hard on all of us who are part of the natural way."

"Is there any area where you've felt her stronger than others?" Lugh asked, hoping his input would help speed things along. He had the general impression Terrabeth wasn't known for her speed in getting things done and if they were going to get home before any of the folks noticed them missing, they weren't going to have a lot of time.

"She stays away from the river," Terrabeth said. "It's only when she calls on it to power her magic that I can feel her." She cocked her head and stared at Lugh. "I believe you have an affinity for water, much like he does." She gestured to Wyn.

Lugh nodded. "I grew up on the beach."

A faraway look filled her orange eyes. "It has been many years since I was at an ocean beach. It would be nice to go there again, but no one summons me these days. It's like summoning has become a lost art among the magic users nowadays."

"There aren't a lot of summoners left, and most of them are Christians of various flavors," Abby said. "I don't know if many people still understand how to do it."

"Is that why you and your mother always invade my home without so much as a knock when you need something out of old Terrabeth?" She looked back at Abby.

"I don't really know." Abby shrugged. "Mother always just comes to see you. I thought it was polite."

Terrabeth huffed. "It's polite when you take time to let me know first. At least when I'm summoned somewhere, I know what's happening and who's calling. When you Magi just show up, I have no clue what's going on or who's coming to see me until you're actually here."

Lugh didn't want to do anything that might upset the troll. It all sounded very complex and strange. He also didn't want to upset his mother by not being where he was supposed to be. "Terrabeth, you say the Elemental witch isn't near the river, so does that mean she's closer to the mountains?" He wished he knew the area around Steamboat Springs better than he did, but since he'd been there only a few months, he was still figuring everything out. He glanced at Wyn, who'd been unusually quiet since they arrived in the grotto.

Terrabeth sighed. "You are a wonder of logic young Magi. It's a wonder the community is afraid of your kind."

From the look on Abby's face, she wasn't expecting to get much more from the troll. "Thanks for the help, Terrabeth. What can we do for you?"

A sudden bolt of fear shot through Lugh. Although Aunt Catherine had never covered talking to trolls, or other fairy folk, Lugh had read a bit on line about fairy tale creatures and how you never make a bargain with them. It always ended up going better for them than it did the humans.

"She really doesn't know when to shut up does she?" Bran mumbled from Lugh's shoulder.

Lugh didn't feel rude not replying to him. He didn't want to risk diverting his attention from Terrabeth.

"Summon me from time to time," Terrabeth sounded lonely. "Let me out to see the world. I keep asking your mother for this and she never complies, but then she always brings me something tasty. You didn't happen to bring me something tasty?"

Abby shook her head. "I knew I was forgetting something."

Terrabeth looked to Lugh and Wyn. "What about you two, did either of you remember to bring something for me to eat?"

Lugh's heart thudded so loudly he could suddenly hear it in his ears. He shook his head. "I'm sorry, Abby didn't tell us we were coming to visit you. She waited until we got to the foot of the bridge to tell us where you lived."

Slowly Terrabeth got to her feet. "Abby, do you think you were being fair to your friends?"

Abby sighed. Even in the short time Lugh had known her, he recognized her exasperated sound. If there was one thing Abby was good at, it was showing drama. "No, Terrabeth, I wasn't being fair, I was trying to get in and out of here as quickly as possible."

"But if friends are being kept in the dark, it isn't fair," Terrabeth snapped. With each word, she seemed to get more agitated. Lugh desperately didn't want to see what happened if she got really mad.

"Mad trolls aren't something we want to mess with," Bran said, echoing Lugh's concerns.

"Look, Terrabeth, this has been a lot of fun, and I appreciate the information." Abby gestured behind her, indicating Lugh should get close so they could make a break for the water path they'd come in on.

Lugh grabbed Wyn's hand and put his hand on Abby's shoulder.

"We're going to get wet again," Bran complained.

"And then you'll get dry." Lugh snapped a little harder than he meant to. It wasn't Bran's fault Terrabeth was getting mad. She was angry with Abby, and Lugh totally understood where she was coming from.

Terrabeth stopped moving. "No need to run away, young Abby. It's been so long since your mother and you came to visit."

Abby shook her head. "Tell you what, we'll either summon you real soon, or we'll come visit again." She made the rune for water. "You have my word." She pushed power through the rune and the path opened up before them.

Lugh didn't have a chance to get a breath before the water flowed over them. He sputtered and hoped he wasn't swallowing too much water, then they were in air again. He sat down heavily on the foot path that crossed at the bridge. Gasping for breath, Lugh wished there was some spell he could cast to let him breathe water. He suddenly wondered if there was, how long it lasted and if it would be able to help him find the place where his father died. If nothing else, he had a lead and that was more than he had before their meeting with Terrabeth. It wasn't much, but it was something.

"That was close," Wyn sputtered as he plopped next to Lugh. "She was scary."

Abby rang water out of her hair. "She's a troll. She's supposed to be scary."

The cats rolled on the grass.

"You know, Abby's the one making deals with the troll," Bran said as he rolled. *"You don't have to go visit her ever again. We can stay dry."*

Lugh swore he was more wet from the return trip than from getting to Terrabeth's grotto. "It wasn't that bad."

Abby sighed. "Well, we at least know where not to look. That leaves the east side of town and the north side. There's rivers along the south side and just to the west."

"Okay, but we should probably get to my house." Lugh forced himself to stand, then offered Wyn a hand up. "If Mom gets home and we're not there, she's going to call your mother and they'll compare notes-"

"And we'll be in trouble," Abby finished for him.

"So we'd better get to Lugh's house," Wyn said as he led them back down the walking paths toward Lugh's place. Lugh wanted to look back over the bridge and see if Terrabeth was there watching for them, and he wondered if he was ever going to be able to walk over a bridge again and not worry about what was living underneath it. He wasn't sure he was going to want to deal with a troll anytime soon.

24

Unwanted Delays

The sky was growing dark by the time they reached Lugh's street.

"I hate the way it gets dark so early." Lugh reached his hand into his pocket for his house keys.

"We're farther north than you're used to," Abby replied. "In a couple of months it'll be dark by five, but it won't last long."

"And the summer days last a lot longer than you're used to," Wyn added.

"The longer days when we got here were nice," Lugh agreed. He had been amazed at the extra hours in the evening. It had made him wonder what it would be like even further north when the summer days were longer, but he wasn't sure how he'd feel about much shorter winter days.

They started up the walk. A soft blue glow appeared on the walk in front of them. Espe was more translucent than normal.

"Lugh, there is danger." Espe and Freida dashed toward them.

"What's going on?" Lugh asked as his heart pounded. The house was dark, but it was still early for his mother to be home. He hoped she was still at work. She'd be safer at work.

"Lady Shadow is attacking Sacred Paths. Catherine needs you."

Abby turned on her heels. "Mom!"

Lugh didn't even stop to think about it, he raced after her, and from the sound of footfalls behind him, Wyn followed them. Bran and Morrigan ran faster, barely pausing at street corners. Lugh was thankful there wasn't much traffic out.

"There's definitely something wrong," Bran said. *"Bast isn't answering our calls. Lugh, we have to hurry."*

"We're running as fast as we can." Lugh skidded to a stop as Abby and Morrigan disappeared in front of him, then he remembered the path that ran down the street. It would be a faster way to get to the shop.

"Bran!" Lugh skidded to a stop. The times he'd accessed the paths while moving had been flukes. He needed to concentrate to access the magic.

Bran turned and dashed back to Lugh, throwing himself into Lugh's arms without pause, then quickly scrambled onto Lugh's shoulder.

"What are you doing?" Wyn asked as he stopped behind Lugh.

"Taking a path," Lugh said in between breaths. He was a lot better than he had been when they first moved to Steamboat, but running or other prolonged excretion still hit him and left him short of breath. He grabbed Wyn's hand. "Come on."

With his free hand, Lugh drew the rune of air and pushed out the power he needed to open the path. The doorway shimmered into existence and Lugh stepped into it, bringing Wyn with him.

"This is always cool," Wyn said as the gray world of the paths closed around them.

"I just wish we did this more when things aren't nuts," Lugh said as he took off with a long stride and the world beyond the path blurred. In front of him, Abby was just a pale shade of her normal self as she raced down the path.

Bright lights illuminated the gray. It was coming from the area near Sacred Paths. Lugh stopped in his tracks. It was obvious a lot of magic was being thrown around.

"Lugh, be careful," Espe said.

"How are you talking to me?" Lugh asked. "We weren't touching when we entered the path."

"I'm a spirit," she said. "The rules are different for me."

Lugh was so tired of learning new rules every time he turned around. He kept hoping there'd be an end to it, but knew he was just starting to understand what it meant to be a Magus. "I don't have time for more rules, we have to help Catherine and Abby." Lugh reversed the rune for air so they could step out of the path and onto the sidewalk a block down from Sacred Paths.

Abby stood a couple doors down with her hands moving rapidly as a protective shield shimmered into existence around her and Morrigan. Before Lugh could do anything, a bolt of energy blasted out of the lengthening twilight. Lugh stared in the direction the bolt had come from. A pair of robed figures stood half a block away. One of them was gesturing in what looked like the start of a spell.

"Wyn, stay close." Lugh focused on his ring and made a protective rune to summon his own protective circle.

"This isn't just Lady Shadow, is it?" Wyn asked.

"It doesn't look that way." Lugh tried to think of what he should do. "There has to be something we can do to help."

"Once the sun is completely down, I can help more." Espe appeared inside the circle. She looked a lot more substantial than she had on the sidewalk outside Lugh's house.

"We still have a few minutes before that," Wyn said. "So the sun affects your power?"

"It affects all spirits." She ran her hand through her long hair. "Actually it affects most forms of magic. That's probably why they attacked when they did."

"So they might just get stronger as the sun goes down." Lugh didn't like thinking that way. It was going to be a hard enough fight without the people they were fighting getting stronger as night deepened.

A bolt of power bounced off Lugh's shield. It lit up the twilight. A bolt of pain lanced through Lugh's skull. He rubbed his head.

"What's wrong?" Wyn asked.

"They're strong," Lugh replied. In all the mock fights he'd had with Catherine and Abby, he'd never felt pain on the level he did when the bolt hit. He didn't know how many strikes he'd be able to hold out against.

"We'll be fine," Bran said. *"Tap into my power. I can feel Abby drawing from Morrigan. I'll tap into more familiar power."*

His energy roared into Lugh. He poured it into his shield. He needed an option. He didn't know enough to protect himself and Wyn. But he had to do something. Lugh threw a bolt of magic toward the robed figures. It was focused, but it bounced off the protections they quickly put up.

"Lugh, use my power too," Wyn said. "It's not as much as you're used to, but I think every little bit will help."

"Thank you." Lugh squeezed his hand. Energy surged through the link they'd developed. Even if it wasn't as strong as what he was used to getting from Bran, it was more than he'd had before.

"Careful not to draw too much of his power," Bran warned. *"He can't take it like I can."*

Lugh took the power and threw it into another bolt of power. It hit their shield just as Abby's bolt hit. The shield flared and then collapsed.

Espe roared out of Lugh's protective circle and shot down the sidewalk. She was little more than a light blue comet racing toward the robed figures. Her familiar was a similar streak beneath her. When she hit, they flew backward, apparently unable to protect themselves from her spirit magic.

With a flourish, Lugh pushed out another force bolt at the robed figures. The one on the right caught the blast full in the face. He stumbled back into the wall of the shop he was standing in front of. Abby got off another blast and it caught the same man, causing him to crumble to the ground.

"Get off me!" the other man screamed as Espe attacked him.

Her body glowed bright as she hit him hard in the face. Over the tops of the buildings, the sky darkened as the sun dropped below the horizon. As it faded, Espe glowed brighter.

Still holding Wyn's hand, Lugh dropped the protective shield and took off toward Abby. "Together!" he shouted.

They'd done some practicing merging their magics; even before they'd fought Lady Shadow, they'd gotten pretty good at it. But normally it was Abby who merged their power. When Lugh touched her shoulder, her power flooded into him. It was stronger than Wyn's. It made him hum with energy. He let that energy fly to the figure Espe fought. It caught them both, and knocked them back into the brick wall. Espe disappeared into the wall. The figure slumped down.

"We have to get to Mom," Abby said, stepping away from Lugh.

"Right with you," Lugh agreed.

In the distance, sirens wailed. Smoke filled the sky coming up from the next block, where Sacred Paths was. Lugh's chest tightened as the three of them with the two familiars ran toward the store. There was a flash of blue and Espe and Frieda were with them. They had to hurry. In his gut, Lugh knew it was more than just the two robed figures. Somewhere Lady Shadow was leading the attack. He knew it. If the two robed figures were Shadow Magi, they'd just found a link between them and Lady Shadow.

25

Into the Smoke

Bran's claws dug into Lugh's shoulder as the cat tried to keep its balance while they ran toward the metaphysical shop. The cat was projecting fear on a level Lugh had never felt before.

"Bran, we have to stay calm, or magic won't work," Lugh said, as much to his familiar as to himself.

"I know. But, something is majorly wrong. Why won't Bast answer me?"

"She's probably busy lending Catherine power." Lugh hoped that was the answer and not something much worse. After losing his father, he'd just found Catherine and Abby. He couldn't stand it if something happened to either one of them, and if something did happen to Catherine, then who was going to finish his and Abby's Magus training?

They slowed to a stop as the smoke billowing from the building grew dense and black. Lugh had never seen so much smoke.

"What are we going to do?" Abby wailed as the sirens grew closer. "Mom's still in there. I know it."

"The smoke won't hurt me," Espe glided past them, Frieda running at her spectral heels. She didn't seem to wait for them to respond. She kept going, disappearing into the smoke.

Somewhere in the building, something exploded. More smoke billowed out.

Then Lady Shadow tumbled out of the smoke, rolling out into the street. Two cars coming down the street screeched to stops, narrowly missing the Elemental witch. Lady Shadow didn't seem to mind. She stood up, shook her head as if to clear it, then gestured with a lot of power toward the burned exterior of the shop.

"No!" Lugh shouted and called up a shield between the Elemental witch and where he presumed Aunt Catherine was.

Lady Shadow's attack hit his shield. Feedback from the blow hit Lugh hard. His head reeled and he sank to his knees, trying desperately to get his thoughts back in order.

"Lugh," Bran's voice in his head was almost too much. *"Come on. Keep going. We can't let her win."*

Gritting his teeth, Lugh forced himself to stand. "We're not going to." Even if the shop was a total loss, he was going to do everything he could to bring Lady Shadow down and save Catherine.

Abby touched his shoulder. "You, Bran, and Wyn keep her occupied. I'm following Espe to find Mom."

Lugh squared his shoulders and readied himself for the next attack.

"Are you sure you two are ready to play in the big leagues?" Lady Shadow taunted as she turned her attention from the shop to Lugh.

"We've dealt with bigger, badder folks than you," Lugh shouted back at her.

She laughed. "The Shadow coven that was here? They were little more than dabblers." She gestured and the ground beneath Lugh's feet shook. "You Magi always think you're so powerful, when all you do is limit yourselves. You don't know real power until it puts you in your grave."

Her monologuing gave Lugh time to get his head cleared and ready an attack. With Wyn and Bran giving him power, he sent a bolt of magic at her. When it struck her hastily constructed shield, she stumbled back a couple of steps. Lugh readied another shot and wished he had another way to attack her. There had to be something beyond just throwing bolts of magical power at her. He suddenly wondered how she'd handle bullets and if that would be considered fair. But wasn't everything fair in war?

A fire truck turned toward them, its siren still blaring. People were gathering on the sidewalks down the block, but from what Lugh could tell, none of them had noticed the magical battle in the middle of the street.

Then the localized earth quake must have reached the onlookers. Someone screamed and folks fled the street. The burning building swayed and the fire truck came to a halt about half a block from where Lugh stood waiting for Lady Shadow's next attack.

"Lugh, let's try something," Wyn whispered in his ear. "Remember Catherine using the invisibility spell? Do you recall the rune for that?"

Lugh's thoughts were jumbled and he tried to recall the lines she'd drawn.

"This is it," Bran sent a picture of the rune into Lugh's mind.

"Okay, got it," Lugh said. "But now what?"

"Cast it. Draw the rune, make us invisible," Wyn said. "Then we can use the smoke as cover and sneak in behind Lady Shadow. Hit her over the head real hard and knock her out. It would work in the movies."

"Sure, let's try it." Hoping keeping hold of Wyn and Bran would let the spell affect them too, Lugh focused on his ring and drew the rune. The plan wasn't a gun, but it was an alternative to just throwing magical bolts at her. It hurt to make the sign in the air and when he finished and put power into it, he nearly fell to his knees with the effort. Like when Catherine had cast it on him, he could still see himself and them.

"Did it work?" Wyn asked.

"I hope so," Lugh replied. "I don't know how much more magic I can do today." His chest hurt and he couldn't seem to get his breath, it made the throbbing in his brain that much worse.

"My Magus is doing great," Bran said. The thought hammered through Lugh's head.

"Bran, my head is killing me. Please be quiet for a little while." At that moment, all Lugh really wanted to do was go find a dark room and go to sleep in hopes his head felt better when he woke up.

"Trying to be invisible again little Magus?" Lady Shadow called out. "With all this smoke for me to work with, it won't help you." She gestured and air power flowed out of her. It made Lugh's head hurt even worse. Then a breeze blew over the fire and the smoke changed course to wash down toward them.

Realizing what she was doing, Lugh froze. When the smoke reached them they'd be outlined in it. She'd be able to know where they were and attack.

Wyn pushed against him. "Go. Now. Before the smoke reaches us."

His urging was just what Lugh needed. Keeping a firm hold on Wyn's hand, he hurried down the street toward the Elemental witch. He wished he had a baseball bat, a club, or something he could hit her with.

"Just use your fist. If we all three hit her at once, maybe we can bring her down," Bran said, his voice soft, like he was trying to limit the level of pain his mind speech caused Lugh.

"Together then." Lugh leaned into his attack, putting his shoulder down so he'd catch her in the back.

Lady Shadow turned just as they hit her. Instead of striking her in the back, Lugh's shoulder caught her in the arm. Bran launched off his shoulder, leaving deep painful scratches as he went for her head. Wyn grabbed her around the waist and together they slammed her into the pavement.

The impact shook Lugh hard, sending stars into his vision.

"Get off me!" she shouted and flailed around.

She wasn't that much taller than Lugh. He wrapped his arms around her and tried to hold on tight, hoping if he immobilized her, she'd be unable to use her magic.

Bran Yowled. Lady Shadow screamed, and blood splashed on Lugh's face. There was the sound of a fist striking flesh and he could only assume Wyn was punching her in the back.

Then a blue glow flowed out of the smoke.

"You have her," Espe said. "Over here, Catherine, the boys have her."

Coughing, Catherine and Abby appeared out of the smoke. "Good work, Lugh, Wyn and you too Bran." Catherine reached down and slipped a necklace over Lady Shadow's head. The necklace screamed of magic, then everything went still. "This should hold her for a while. Now we all need to get out of here before this becomes too much for the humans to ignore. Luckily I've got wards around the shop to prevent non-magical folks from noticing anything strange that might happen around here. But those will fail as soon as the fire consumes the building." She grabbed Lady Shadow by the hair and hauled her to her feet. "Let's go." She dragged Lady Shadow away until they reached a path they could access, then they all headed to her house. All the fight seemed to have instantly gone out of Lady Shadow, unless that was part of the necklace's magic.

Being drained of magic and his head pounding, it was all Lugh could do to make the trip. As it was he stumbled as they cleared the path into Catherine and Abby's back yard. Wyn caught him and lowered him to the ground.

"Rest a few minutes," Wyn said. "You have thrown around a whole lot of magic."

"I know." Lugh's voice came out a harsh whisper. Then he let his eyelids close. Somewhere in the distance, he heard his mother start shouting. He smiled slightly. At least she wasn't shouting at him.

176

26

Waking up Tired

Lugh rubbed his head and sat up. He was in a bed, but the room didn't smell or look like his. Everything was dark. There was a soft lavender smell to the place and he wrinkled his nose. Soft instrumental music was playing in the background and someone was snoring. It felt like his pillow and his bed. It was more than a little disorienting.

"You're awake." Bran said, then yawned.

Thankfully his thoughts didn't make Lugh's head hurt. "I think so. How long was I asleep?"

"Almost a day." The bed moved and Lugh realized Bran was curled up next to his legs. *"I need to go get your mother. I had to promise I'd do that as soon as you woke up."*

"Wait a minute, how did you do that?" Lugh was sure it was impossible for Bran to speak to his mother. "She can't hear you."

"And I'm very thankful for that." Bran paused at the foot of the bed. *"Although, maybe if she could, she'd get me the cat food I like as opposed to what she thinks I'll eat. But anyway, Bast and Catherine helped me negotiate with her so she'd go get some rest. She and Wyn*

have been here since we got back. Wyn is more stubborn than she is. I wasn't sure that was possible." He jumped off the bed and disappeared.

Lugh wasn't sure it was possible for Wyn to be more stubborn than his mother, and if that was the case, he worried that his life with Wyn might be more complicated than he expected.

There was a shift in the snoring, then silence. "Hey, Lugh," Wyn whispered. "Did I just hear you talking with Bran?"

"Yeah." Lugh said. His throat was dry enough he wished he had a cup of water.

"Good. You've been out for a while." The bed shifted and Wyn's arms wrapped around him. "I was starting to get worried."

"You were asleep." Lugh said.

Wyn kissed Lugh's cheek. "I was worried before I fell asleep to have dreams of how worried I was."

A light came on in the hall seconds before Bran jumped on the bed.

His mother looked tired as she stopped just inside the doorway. "You're awake."

"Yeah, but I'm still tired." Lugh didn't bother fighting the yawn that slipped out.

With swift steps, his mother made it to the bed side. "You had me very worried." She laid her hand on his forehead like she expected him to have a fever. "If we hadn't just gone through this with Abby, I'd have had you in the hospital, but Catherine assured me it was just you using too much magic."

"I didn't realize it was going to wear me out so much." Lugh could never remember feeling so tired in his life. If he closed his eyes, he was pretty sure he'd just go instantly back to sleep.

She shook her head and sat down on the bed, opposite Wyn. "I wish you wouldn't do things like this."

Lugh managed to not roll his eyes at her. "Mom, I don't have much choice, it's who I am now."

She put her finger on his lips to quiet him. "I know that, sweetie. Catherine told me how you, Wyn and Bran brought Lady Shadow down. That was very brave of you."

"I had help." He rolled his head slightly so he lay his check against Wyn's.

"*I was there too,*" Bran lay on Lugh's pillow, catching just a bit of his hair on his way and accidently pulling it.

"You were all very brave." She reached up to pet Bran before ruffling Wyn's hair like his father always did.

"Thanks," Wyn said softly as color rose in his cheeks.

"What's happened while I've been sleeping?" Lugh hoped they'd gotten the fire under control, and still had Lady Shadow out of commission.

His mother shook her head. "The store's a complete loss, along with all the shops in that block. Lady Shadow is dangerous."

"Is?" Wanting to know what happened, Lugh tried to get out of bed and go find Catherine, but his mother and Wyn held him in place.

"She's not a danger right now," Wyn said. "Catherine called some of the other Magi and they've taken her off somewhere. It's all really hush hush. But the two guys in robes got away. Catherine couldn't find any trace of them where we left 'em."

"So, we don't know who they were?" Lugh really wanted to get everything worked out so there were answers, but he doubted that was going to happen. With magic, it was too easy for things and people to slip between the cracks and just disappear.

His mother shook her head. "No. That they know where to find you all worries me, but Catherine is doing everything she can to keep us all safe. Unfortunately she keeps telling me there's nothing we can really do but wait for them to appear again."

Lugh hated the idea of waiting, but he knew they were right. Without knowing who or even what the two figures were, there was little they could do until they showed up again. The idea of it made him even more tired than he had been before. "Are Catherine, Abby, Morrigan and Bast all right?"

"They all have a bit of smoke damage to their throats and lungs, but nothing time won't heal," his mother said. "It's a good thing I'm a nurse, or they might've had to go to the ER. That was a very nasty fire. The fire department has declared it was old gas pipes, and the earthquake was just part of the pipes going."

"Because people look for easy explanations," Wyn added. "It's what makes magic so easy to hide."

"And a lot of us just resist accepting those things we can't easily explain," Lugh's mother said, then sighed. "Do you need anything? You've been asleep long enough; you should probably eat something."

As she said it, Lugh's stomach rumbled, and he moved and his bladder complained. "Yeah. I know it's nighttime, but can I have breakfast? Pancakes sound great."

Nodding, his mother stood. "Pancakes it is. Come into the kitchen in a couple of minutes and they'll be ready. I'll call Catherine and let her know you're awake." She hurried out the door.

Lugh gave Wyn a quick kiss. "I need to hit the bathroom."

Wyn hugged him. "I could be evil and hold you here in the bed, but I need to go too."

"Then let me up." Lugh laughed and pushed at Wyn.

"What, don't you want me to be able to tell your mother you still wet the bed?" Wyn hugged him tighter, then let go.

"You'd better not." Lugh laughed again as he made it a couple of steps away from Wyn. They'd been through a lot, but he was still alive, Bran was still alive and so were Wyn and everyone else. He'd learned how dangerous magic could be early on, and was just thankful they'd all made it through safe and sound. The fatigue he felt was nothing a bit of sleep couldn't resolve.

A. M. Burns

27

Late Samhain

A fresh coating of snow made the drive up the mountain a lot more hazardous than it had been the first two times Lugh had gone with Catherine and Abby for the holiday gathering of the local Magi. When they reached the trailhead parking, Lugh zipped up his coat as Bran jumped up onto his shoulder.

"Not walking tonight?" Lugh asked. Normally Bran raced along the trail with Bast and Morrigan as they hurried to the meeting place so they could talk with the other familiars.

"I think this time I'll ride with you," Bran curled around the back of Lugh's neck so he was mostly inside the hood of his coat.

Lugh had to admit, the extra warmth Bran provided was welcome, but he wasn't going to let him off the hook that easily. "I think you're cold."

Abby laughed as she pulled one of the back packs they always carried out of the back of the SUV. "Of course he's cold. He's still a kitten. When he gets older he'll be more apt to run along with the others, unless the snow is too deep."

"I am not cold," Bran snapped. *"I just seek to provide my Magus with more comfort on our way to the circle."*

He sounded so convincing, Lugh couldn't help but laugh. "Yeah, I'm glad this is for my comfort."

"Everything I do is to help you," Bran said, and shifted slightly as Lugh shouldered the pack he'd carry.

"Anyone need anything else?" Catherine asked as she reached to close the rear door.

"I'm good," Abby said.

"Me too," Lugh added.

"Good. Let's get moving, sun's going down quickly." Catherine slammed the door closed before turning down the trail that would lead them up the mountain to their special spot for group magic.

As they reached the bend in the trail where they could see the lights of Steamboat Springs sparkling below them, two large birds swooped down toward them.

Bran pushed his head out of Lugh's hood and stared at them. *"It's Matilda and Gray!"*

Lugh nodded. He recognized the two familiars from previous circles. That meant at least a couple of the other Magi had made it, even if there hadn't been any other vehicles in the trailhead parking lot. Mark Manford, and Henry Claiborne, the two Magi who had the hawk and owl familiars, must've used the paths to get to the circle. The major east/west air path went right through their circle site.

Another bend in the turn and they could spot four people standing around a roaring bonfire. Lugh figured that meant

Cybil Claiborne, Henry's daughter who was just a couple years older than he and Abby, had made it and probably Tom Smith, a Magus who had a ferret familiar. After Bran reporting a ferret at the house where the Shadow Magi had taken Abby and Wyn, Lugh had wondered if Tom was really one of the good guys. But he had been at the Equinox circle in September, so Lugh hadn't had the opportunity to get more information. It would've been nice if Bran could've identified Tom's ferret Fierce as the one at the house, but the longer they went without seeing Tom, the less chance Bran would be able to be sure it was the same scent and not just a ferret.

"That's not Tom," Bran said from Lugh's hood. *"It's a girl. We've never met her before. I think that gray lump at her feet is her familiar, it smells a bit like a cat, but not exactly."*

A new Magus. Lugh couldn't wait to meet her.

"Ah, there you are," Mark said, coming up to hug Catherine. "We were beginning to wonder if the snow was too deep for you."

Kissing his cheek, Catherine laughed. "Takes a lot more snow than that to keep us home. If it had been too bad, we'd have just taken the path up here, but I like the drive."

"Right. Don't want to deny you something you enjoy." Henry joined in. "Well come over here you three, you need to meet my newest apprentice, Leslie Falk."

Leslie was a slender girl who looked to be about Lugh's age. Her hair peeking out from under her wool hat was a soft blonde with gentle red highlights. "Hi." She waved shyly. "Oh, I'm supposed to introduce my familiar, this is Silky."

Silky stood and stretched. She was a large cat with tufts on her ears. Lugh tried to figure out what she was. She didn't look like any house cat he'd ever seen.

"A lynx," Abby said. "Wow, did you call a lynx? Oh, I'm Abby, by the way and Morrigan is my familiar."

"Call a lynx?" Leslie tilted her head and looked confused. "Silky found me."

"Leslie doesn't come from a recent Magus family," Henry said as Matilda landed on the leather reinforced patch on his shoulder. "From what I've been able to figure out, the last Magus in her family was about two hundred years ago."

Catherine's eyes grew wide. "That's unusual."

Henry nodded. "There's a lot of unusual stuff going on right now. You've seen that yourself."

"Right. I think this is the first time in years, we've had a holiday circle a few days late, but there was too much going on. So, have any of you been able to track down any of the Magi who used to be in Colorado Springs?" Catherine asked.

Henry and Mark both shook their heads. "Coming up with nothing, and there's not been any new Magi move into the area. I can't believe that happened without any of us realizing it before now."

A soft blue light grew brighter as Espe materialized near the fire. "The darkness has been building for a while."

Mark's eyes grew wide and he paled. "Espe? Espe Colman? What happened to you?"

"I was killed on the path, Mark Manford. It is sad to see how old all of you have gotten." Espe frowned.

"Time impacts all of us," Henry replied before Mark could. "But why are you here? You shouldn't be here."

"From what we can figure, Colin cast a spell to call a guardian for Lugh if something happened to him," Catherine explained. "It took a while before she was pulled back to this plane on a constant basis and then pulled to Lugh."

"When she first found me, she thought I was Dad." Lugh added. Even though he'd been taught to not butt in on adults' conversations, he felt this was more his tale to tell than Catherine's and the older Magi were always telling the younger ones they were to be treated as equals. "It took her a few nights to realize I wasn't him."

"You do look a lot like your father did when he was your age, which was when Espe disappeared." Henry rubbed his chin. "So I guess the question is, what are we going to do with you, Espe?"

"I want to keep guarding Lugh." She put her hands on her hips and glared at Henry. "I think it's what Colin would've wanted."

"But you're denying yourself your eternal rest," said Cybil Claiborne, Mark's daughter.

Espe shrugged. "Other than when I was called to help Magi in trouble, I can't remember where I've been since I was killed. I barely remember being killed. If that's the eternal rest I'm missing out on, I don't see what the big deal is. At least here, I'll be doing something and making memories."

Lugh nodded. "I agree. If she wants to stay around, I say we let her. Where is the harm in it? Not to mention she proved in the fights with Lady Shadow that she can pull her own weight in fighting the darkness." He knew that he, Wyn and Abby had at first talked about doing something on Samhain to help Espe find her rest, but if she didn't want that, he didn't think they should push it on her. It didn't seem fair or right.

Henry shook his head. "Trying to lay a spirit to rest who doesn't want to go takes a lot of power. Espe, if you're sure you want to stay, I think the light workers can use a hand right now." He glanced at Leslie and Silky as the other cats, except Bran, were approaching and welcoming the lynx. "There are strange things going on right now and the light needs all the help it can get."

Catherine frowned. "If you stay, Espe, we're going to need to sit down and come up with some ground rules as to what you can and cannot do."

Espe nodded. "That's fine, Catherine. I do understand that I'm new and different from what I was when you knew me twenty-five years ago."

Frieda bounded from Espe's side to join the other familiars in greeting Silky.

Bran sighed. *"I suppose I should go and meet her too. It really is nice and warm in your hood."*

Lugh pushed his hood down to make it easier for Bran to get out. "Go be nice to everyone else."

"Okay, but if I get cold, I'm getting back in your hood." Bran bounced over to see the others. *"Maybe Silky will have some mousing pointers. She has to be a good hunter."*

Lugh smiled and lifted his hood back over his head. His life had changed a lot since coming to Steamboat Springs. He'd found magic, his extended family, a boyfriend, magical friends, a guardian spirit and most of all Bran. Sure, there was danger and the unexpected, but as he got more and more used to it, he found he enjoyed not knowing what was coming each day. That just gave him more reason to get out of bed and see what was going to happen.

The End

Familiar Spirit

Familiar Magic
By A·M· Burns

1

A Windy Walk

The wind hit Lugh McNeal hard as he walked out of the house. He shivered and ducked his head deeper into the heavy collar of his coat. For two weeks, the wind had been howling like he'd never encountered before, even though everyone assured him it was perfectly normal for late winter in Steamboat Springs, Colorado, he wasn't sure he liked it. He wanted to be able to head out and not worry about getting frostbite before he reached the car, and the idea of walking several blocks to his boyfriend's house was daunting. Being from Florida, his first real winter in Colorado was a major wakeup call to the incredible difference between the life he'd known and the one he had after his father died. Everything was vastly changed. He wasn't a normal kid anymore, he was a Magi, and could command powerful magical forces with the help of his cat familiar Bran. He wasn't a beach kid anymore, but hadn't taken to snow skiing the way a lot of the locals did. Snow skiing was vastly different from water skiing, which he was only passable at.

"We could stay home and let Wyn come to us," Bran, Lugh's familiar said from his spot inside Lugh's hood. The cat's warmth help keep the chill off Lugh's neck.

"We've been doing that way too much lately." Lugh paused at the curb and checked for on-coming traffic. Thankfully there weren't many cars out, even though it was Saturday and there should've been a lot of folks out and about.

"He never complains." Bran snuggled a bit deeper in an obvious effort to avoid the wind. *"He's used to this weather."*

"And we'll get used to it, if we're out in it." Lugh took out across the park that was across the street from his house. It was the most direct route to Chambers' Mountain Gear the shop Wyn's family owned down by the Yampa River. The snow there made the going a little slow, but he and some of the other more adventurous neighbors had made a pretty clear path diagonally across the center of the open space.

"You do realize that most sensible cats stay inside during the worst parts of winter." Bran's tail flicked, hitting Lugh in the ear.

"Then you should be lucky you aren't as sensible as most." Lugh was thankful there weren't many people out in the weather as he entered the tourist section of town. He didn't have to worry about people looking at him strangely as he apparently conversed with no one. If there had been a lot of people around, he'd have responded to Bran telepathically, but since he'd grown up verbally speaking everything, it just made things easier. He was still getting used to using telepathy with the cat, and sometimes he had trouble thinking and walking at the same time.

"I am a familiar." Bran's tail flicked a little more constantly, revealing his agitation. *"I should be more sensible than most cats. I have to look after you, my Magi, and keep you alive."*

"And you do a very admirable job of that too." Sometimes Lugh wondered who Bran worried about more, himself or Lugh, but the cat was always there when he needed him for an extra boost in his magic, or needed more information. All familiars could tap into their family knowledgebase, making it very impressive how much Bran knew, even though he wasn't a year old yet.

"Bast would be very disappointed in me if I didn't do my best. I can't disappoint my mother." Bast was Lugh's Aunt Catherine's familiar and the mother of several familiars of the local Magi.

The wind picked up as they stopped at the corner of Lincoln Avenue. Lugh shivered as did Bran. The only time he'd experienced winds like what he endured that winter was the time he'd followed his father out to close up a shed door that had flown open during a hurricane. He bowed his head and kept going when the light turned and he could cross the street. More than once, he'd asked Aunt Catherine if he could learn a few spells to help combat the weather, and she'd explained how it could be dangerous if he went around manipulating the natural world too much. If he tried to still the wind near himself just to make things easier, the energy had to go somewhere and the winds would hit somewhere close by harder, making things worse for other people. One of the things Magi learned early on was they had to endure so others could be protected, and if that meant he had to learn to live with the wind trying to blow him and Bran down the street as he hurried across, then that's what he had to do.

A block south of Lincoln Avenue, sat Chambers' Mountain Gear. During the summer, they did a lot of kayak rentals and hiking gear, in the winter is was skis, snowboards, snowshoes, and winter wear. It was always a hub of activity in Steamboat. But the time Lugh made it through the back door, he wasn't sure if he was going to be able to feel his nose ever again. He kicked the bit of snow off his boots. For the amount of snow they'd gotten during the heart of winter, he was always amazed how well the city kept the streets and sidewalks cleared. He'd only gotten snow on him when he'd crossed the park.

Before he'd gotten the snow off his boots, a yipping filled the back room as a small red dog came racing in.

"Ruby, it's just me." Lugh bent over to let the little Pomeranian sniff his hand.

Bran shifted on his back. *That dog is extremely irritating. I don't understand why she can't just stalk us and then make her presence known. All the yipping isn't a very effective hunting method.*

Lugh couldn't help but laugh as Ruby finally stopped barking and settled in to licking his fingers. "She is who she is."

"Is Bran complaining about Ruby again?" Wyn asked, coming through the opening that led into the front of the shop.

"Always." Lugh straightened from greeting Ruby and smiled. Wyn often made him smile, just by being around and being his boyfriend.

Wyn gave him a big hug and quick kiss. "Glad you came over. Things are a bit slow around here today. What do you say we go take a stroll along the river? Dad says the back country is still too unstable for him to take us up there for a hike, but we could take the path along the river."

Although Lugh would've preferred to park themselves in front of their laptops and get in some gaming, it had been a while since they took a hike, and it would help him get more used to being outside in the wind. "Sure, that'll be fun."

"Right." Wyn reached into Lugh's hood and gave Bran a quick scratch. "Actually, I don't know why, but I've had the urge all day to go take a walk down by the river."

Lugh looked at Wyn. "An urge?" On his last birthday, Lugh had woken up with the urge to go to the river and found Bran there clinging for his life on a rock. It had been the start of his life as a Magi.

Wyn shook his head. "I don't think it's like that. But I've just been feeling cooped up inside today. I need to get out and see what's going on in the world. I think it's more cabin fever than anything else." He strolled over to the line of coat hooks by the back door and grabbed his. "I told Mom we'd be heading that way when you got here. She's cool with it."

"Okay." Lugh was learning how open the Chambers family was to everything. They were Wiccans and incredibly laidback about magic as well as his and Wyn's relationship. It was a vast difference from his own mother who was cool with him being gay, but still had issues with him being a Magi, even though his father had been a Magi. Magic still scared her. She didn't understand things like urges, not the way Wyn's folks did.

"Would you like a couple?" Wyn held up a pair of foil-wrapped packages. They weren't something Lugh even knew existed until a few months earlier, when during their first hike in the snow, Wyn had broken out handwarmers and made Lugh put them in his gloves.

"Sure." Lugh didn't like admitting weakness around Wyn, but he was willing to add a little level of comfort if they were going to head back into the wind.

"It's colder by the river," Bran complained as they crossed the bridge to the south shore.

"No debate here," Lugh replied, careful to keep his thoughts to himself and Bran. He didn't want Wyn knowing the weather was getting to him. He wondered if, once Aunt Catherine taught him some fire magic, if he'd be able to stay warmer on his own.

Wyn paused for a moment as she reached the south shore trail. He looked east and west. "West I think."

"At least it isn't into the wind," Bran grumbled.

"Okay." Lugh stayed next to Wyn as they walked. The first few times he'd been down by the river, there had been a constant stream of walkers and joggers on the trail, and there had been kayaks and canoes on the river, but that afternoon, it was just him and Wyn. If it hadn't been so cold, it would've been really nice. Normally they had to go up into the mountains to get a solitary walk, and they could only do that when Wyn's father had time to drive them up there. One of the things they were both looking forward to was getting drivers licensees in the summer so they could have a lot more freedom.

"So did you get all your homework done last night?" Wyn asked.

"Yeah. Didn't have much. Plus, I wanted the weekend to be open, so we could do whatever we wanted to do." Lugh didn't bother reiterating his mother's hard, fast rule about him finishing up his homework before he could get on the phone with Wyn every night. She said she didn't want his school work falling behind just because he had a boyfriend.

Wyn took his hand, although their gloves muffled the sensation of his touch, it still warmed Lugh in ways the handwarmers could never do. "Good. I wanted to nice quiet weekend too. Since we had midterms last week, we deserve some quiet time."

"Definitely. And it's a good way to start spring break." But he didn't add it didn't feel like spring. It was still cold. In Florida, the flowers would already be pushing their way out of the ground and things would be warm and bright. So far in Steamboat, the only thing he noticed that happened was more skiers coming to town. They were all acting like it was the last opportunity they were going to get to ski, even if the locals were saying the ski resort up the mountain was likely to stay open until at least May thanks to the high snow levels.

Wyn stopped and looked down the riverbank.

"What?" Lugh asked, but a strange magical tingle started dancing along his skin.

"There's something down there." Wyn let go of his hand and stepped off the path

Lugh stared toward the river. There was a large amount of ice along the banks and only a narrow passage of water was near the center of the river. "I don't see anything but ice." But he knew Wyn had felt the same magic he'd felt, but the way he was acting it was stronger.

"I don't know what it is." Wyn slid a bit as he headed toward the ice.

"We could stay here and wait for him to climb back up," Bran said.

"No." Lugh started after Wyn. There was no way he was going to let Wyn get into something when he could be there and lend a hand if things went wrong. One thing he'd learned since becoming a Magi, if there was magic involved, there was a chance for things to go wrong.

Familiar Magic
Coming Soon

ABOUT THE AUTHOR

A.M. BURNS has been writing to pass the time since high school. The stories he wrote helped him deal with life. A few years ago, he started sharing those stories with friends who enjoyed them and he has started sending his works out into the world to share with other people. He lives in the mountains with his extremely supportive husband. They have a lot of critters, including dogs, cats, birds, horses, and rabbits. When not writing, A.M. spends a lot of time hiking, trail riding, or just driving in the mountains. Nature provides a lot of inspiration for his work and keeps him writing. He is also an avid photographer and falconer. Don't get him started talking about his birds, because he won't stop for a while.

Web contact info:
Website: www.amburns.com
Twitter: AM_Burns
Facebook: www.facebook.com/authoramburns
Goodreads author page:
www.goodreads.com/author/show/5134598.A_M_Burns
Pintrest: pinterest.com/mystichawker/
Amazon Author Page: www.amazon.com/-/e/B0054EVI6W

Mystichawker Press Author Page:
http://www.mystichawker.com/amburns.html

More Books From A.M. Burns:

After his family is killed by thieves, sole survivor Trey McAlister is taken in by a nearby Comanche clan. Trey has a gift for magic and the clan s shaman, Singing Crow, makes him an apprentice. While learning to control his powers, Trey bonds with a young warrior and shape shifter, Gray Talon. When they are sent out on a quest to find the missing daughter of a dragon, they encounter the same bandits who murdered Trey s family, as well as a man made of copper who drives Trey to dig deeper into the magics that created him.

It doesn't take them long to discover a rancher near Cheyenne, Wyoming is plotting to build a workforce of copper men and has captured the dragon s daughter they've been searching for. Trey and Gray Talon must draw on all their knowledge and skills to complete their quest one that grows more complicated, and more dangerous, with each passing day."

From DSP Publishing
Available on Amazon.com
And most other places books are sold.

Bigfoot hunters prowl the forests of Cripple Creek, Colorado. That doesn't sit well with Thom Woodmen-a Bigfoot-albeit the runt of his family. Being the smallest has advantages; Thom, in disguise, gets to attend high school, and he's not expected to accomplish much in life. All that changes when he comes across a distressed human in the forest.

Ben Steele is new to Cripple Creek High School, and after a harrowing experience in the woods near his new home, he quickly falls in with Thom Woodmen and his circle of friends. So what if they like to hang out with nature? Ben's got nothing better to do. Trouble is, Ben can't seem to stay out of it-trouble, that is.

However, in saving young Ben's life, Thom inadvertently kick-starts a bonding process that'll change both their lives forever. With the support of family and friends, Thom learns to accept bonding with the human boy. But with the danger overrunning Cripple Creek lately, Thom may be cut down before he can confess his secret and his love.

From Harmony Ink
Available on Amazon.com
And most other places books are sold.

Lugh's mother packed up and moved them from sunny Florida to tiny Steamboat Springs, Colorado after his father's accidental drowning. Resigned to his mom having to work a lot, and only just beginning to deal with his dad's death, Lugh is disappointed when she is called in to work on his fifteenth birthday.

After an unnerving dream, he decides to head to the nearby river where he ends up following a strange, urgent, internal pull. When another boy helps him rescue a young cat from the river, Lugh discovers a family secret he never suspected. Now, with his new cousin Abby and their friend Wyn, Lugh must figure out the rules of his new life before the forces that seek to destroy them can get the upper hand.